THE BOY AND THE GUNFIGHTER

The Weston family left their boy Frank in college and went West to their farm in Colorado. Then a bunch of crooked lawmen killed his family to get their land. Frank went West, hired a gunhand to side him, and learned the art of gunfighting. When he cornered the bushwhackers who had shot up his folks he gave them a short trial and a long rope in a court presided over by Judge Colt.

THE BOY AND THE GUNFIGHTER

Spencer Knight

GUNSMOKE

WESTERNS

First published 1979
by Manor Books, Inc

This hardback edition 1989
by Chivers Press
by arrangement with
Manor Books, Inc

ISBN 0 86220 924 2

British Library Cataloguing in Publication Data

Knight, Spencer
  The boy and the gunfighter.
  I. Title
813'.54 [F]

ISBN 0–86220–924–2

Printed and bound in Great Britain by
Redwood Burn Limited, Trowbridge, Wiltshire

CHAPTER ONE

The moisture from the storms of late March and early April had awakened the slumbering plant life of the high plains. During the long, dry winter there had been little touches of green only along the small stream and in the low-lying areas where underground water seeped to the surface. Now, with the spring rains, the willows and cottonwoods which lined that same stream were beginning to leaf out and the lighter green of the gramma and buffalo grasses was gradually spreading to cover all the land the farmers had not yet begun to work.

The moist blackness of freshly turned earth spread in a patchwork away from the abrupt eastern face of a tall hill. The hill marked the end of a spine of jagged rock which extended for miles across the plains. Low ridges ran away from this spine like the fingers of an open hand and separated the individual farms more distinctly than fences ever could.

The farm which nestled close at the foot of the hill sparkled in the afternoon sun, the buildings fresh with paint, the fences in perfect shape. Unlike most of the farms in a part of Colorado which had just begun to be settled, this one showed signs of a great deal of money.

A half mile from the house in a field beside the road to Singleshoe the farmer was guiding a plow drawn by a team of heavy draft horses, the furrows rolling out straight and even behind him. In the pasture near the streams which separated this farm from the next, a small boy and his dog were tending to a herd of cows. Closer to the house the hired man worked at clearing a large field of its natural growth of prairie grasses and soapweed in preparation for its first planting.

Around the farmyard itself, evidence of the industry of the women could be seen in the occasional appearance of one or another of the three on her way to the barn or one of the other outbuildings. From an upstairs window of the large house the head of a dust mop would appear, be shaken vigorously and disappear back into the dim interior. Spring was a time for clearing away the dust and closeness of winter, a time when everything began anew.

A group of horsemen rode into view along the road from Singleshoe, the town which served the farms of the area as a shopping center. They paused to talk with the farmer. After a short discussion he unhitched the plow and led the team across to the shade of several trees which grew along the fence line. He left them cropping at the grass. He walked alongside the mounted men as they rode towards the house. A wave of his arm brought the hired man over to join them.

As they turned through the gate from the road into the wide farmyard a pretty girl of sixteen came out on the porch and shaded her eyes with a small hand to see who they were. She seemed pleased at the prospect of company and turned to call through the open door behind her. As the men drew to a halt in front of the gate in the white picket fence which surrounded the house, her mother joined her. A dark-haired girl, older by a couple of years than her sister, leaned out a second-floor window, a dust mop still in her hand.

Franklin Weston had talked cheerfully to the man on the horse beside him all during the walk in from where he had been plowing. He called to his wife: "Agnes. Henry has stopped by to see those extra horses we have. He has been looking for some spare mounts for his men and Cam Luck at the livery suggested he try us."

His wife wiped her hand on her apron and smiled a greeting at the men. "Would you like something cool to drink, Sheriff Carr? I'm sure you and your men must be hot from your ride."

Henry Carr removed his spotless white hat when he replied. "Just a drink from your well will be enough, Agnes. I have a number of places to visit today so I want to get right out and look at those horses. With all the arson that's been going on around the valley we have been on the move constantly these last few weeks. It has about worn our horses down."

His men had followed the hired man across to the well and were taking turns drinking from a bucket of cool, fresh water. Their horses lined up at the trough beside the barn for their own refreshment.

Two of the men wandered into the barn while a third investigated the storage shed and the small house where the hired men lived. They were all back out in the open before anyone except the girl at the second-floor window noticed.

Her shoes clattered on the stairs and she burst out onto the porch to ask, "Why are they looking in all the buildings, Dad? Is something wrong?"

The smile on Carr's face faded and he slowly replaced his hat on his head. "You are much too observant, young Miss Weston." At a signal one of his men pulled his gun and held it on the hired man.

Weston watched this in surpries and then turned to demand of the Sheriff, "What is going on, Henry?"

"We didn't come out here about horses," the Sheriff responded coldly. "I came to deliver a message from your neighbors around the valley."

Weston kept his eyes fixed on the Sheriff as he stated firmly, "If anyone in this valley has something to say to me, they know where I live."

"This is a message they want to make real sure you understand. They asked me to deliver it in person so you would know how serious they are."

The same two men as before were now driving the stock out of the barn into the home corral. The hired man watched helplessly, his anger making his face flush red as he cried, "What are you doing with those animals?"

Weston started across the yard towards the barn. The Sheriff moved to block his path with his horse. "You just stay where you are, Weston. I think you want to listen to what I have to say and listen good."

Unable to get past the horse Franklin Weston stepped back to the gate in the picket fence. "What is it you want of us?" he demanded angrily.

"You are a real educated man, Weston. Went to college back east, know all kinds of important people. Makes you look down on your neighbors, doesn't it?"

"It does nothing of the kind and you know it," he replied angrily. "They are all good people. Most of them have been in my home and I've been in theirs."

"That's not the way they see it. To them it looks like you think you're better than they are with all your money and education and fine manners. They've finally had all they can stand of you and your high-tone ways. They want me to tell you that you have until dawn tomorrow to leave this part of the country for good. After that they will have to take more serious action if you are still here."

Franklin Weston was speechless for a moment. When he was finally able to reply he had to struggle to control the emotion in his voice. "I don't believe you, Carr. None of the farmers in this valley told you to tell me anything of the kind. I think this is more of what has been going on all winter. Families leaving never to be heard of again, barns being burned, men riding across the valley in gangs at night shooting at houses." He glanced at the corral. "That is why you have driven the animals out of my barn, isn't it? So you can burn it?"

He stepped forward until he was almost touching Carr's boot. "I suppose you came around with your deputies to give these others a message from their neighbors also. Well it won't work with me! I have no intention of being driven out of my home!"

The Sheriff sat and looked down at him for a long moment, his hands folded calmly across the saddle horn. An anticipatory smile slowly spread across his face. "I believe you just called me a liar, Weston." He drew his revolver and pointed it at the farmer's head. "I don't take kindly to that."

Agnes Weston ran out to her husband's side. "He isn't armed. If you shoot him it will be murder!"

"He would be smart if he didn't push me that far, Agnes. Then I would have to shoot you and your girls so there wouldn't be any witnesses." He looked around at his men. "Get on with it."

The elder daughter stepped to the front of the porch. "You can't do this," she said angrily. "It isn't right."

Carr chuckled. "There sure are a lot of people in this family who want to tell me what I can and can't do. I think if I were in your position I would keep my pretty mouth shut."

Smoke began to appear at the doors and windows of the large barn and soon they could hear the crackling as the flames caught in the heavy wooden beams and began to blaze fiercely.

"Now you know I mean business," the Sheriff said dangerously. "You pack up whatever you intend to take with you and be out of the valley by first light tomorrow. Don't go through town and don't stop until you're well away from the Singleshoe country. It just plain wouldn't be healthy. I don't think I would do any talking about my little visit here today, either. If word gets back to me you have, I'll send a few of my boys to wherever you are and finish you off."

He gestured with the revolver, "Show some sense, Franklin. You can't fight all of us. Take my advice and get out while your family is still in one piece." He leaned forward, his voice cold. "Me and the boys will be back at sunup tomorrow. If we find you still here, someone will get hurt."

His eyes glistened meaningfully as he added, "If I had two daughters looked like your's, I sure wouldn't want to take any chances."

Weston was speechless as he stared up at the man.

A shot rang out from beside the barn and a couple of the men laughed. The dog which had been playing with the boy in the field lay on the hard-packed dirt near the barn. Though its hindquarters had been shattered it was still attempting to drag itself into the burning barn.

"You didn't have to shot the boy's dog," Weston said hopelessly. "Her pups are in there. They can't get out by themselves."

Carr shrugged. "Doesn't matter much now. They must be dead by this time."

The back door of the house slammed and they could hear someone running around the side. The small boy came into view carrying a shotgun nearly as long as he was tall. He stopped, put the gun to his shoulder and fired it in the direction of the man who had shot his dog. The recoil from the gun knocked him sideways and the buckshot passed through the empty air.

"Jimmy! No!" his mother cried in dispair.

The boy regained his balance, broke open the gun and groped in his pocket for shells with which to reload. His movements seemed very slow as his anxious family watched in horror from the front of the house. The gunman who had shot his dog started forward to take the shotgun away from him. As he drew near the weapon clicked shut and the muzzle came up.

It was point-blank range. Even the small boy couldn't miss.

The man shot him in the chest, the impact of the shell against his bones flinging the small body backwards to lie in a twitching heap.

His mother started across the yard towards him.

The gunman heard the sound of the footsteps pounding across the hard-packed dirt behind him.

Already horrified at killing the small boy, he pivoted in sudden panic and shot the mother.

She stopped, stared down in surprise at the hole in her dress over her left breast through which blood was already beginning to seep, raised her hand to touch the wound and slowly slumped to the ground.

Franklin Weston made a desperate lunge for the man on the horse above him. A bullet from the Sheriff's gun struck him square in the face. He slammed into the neck of the turning horse and rebounded to lie motionless on the ground just outside the gate in the picket fence.

The two girls stared in horror from the porch, shock holding them frozen where they stood.

The Sheriff ordered crisply, "Kill the hand. We can't leave any witnesses to this." The man began to run desperately through the group which surrounded him. Fire from a number of guns dropped him first to his knees and then onto his face where he lay dead only a few feet from the faintly struggling dog.

The younger girl reacted first. She grabbed her sister by the hand and pulled her back through the front door which she slammed and locked behind them.

One of the men asked hopefully, "There ain't no need to kill them right now is there, Henry? It had been a good long time since I had a woman looked like either of those."

Carr nodded in silent agreement and the man started up the front walk. The Sheriff called after him, "Weston's neighbors are going to be getting here real soon to see what the smoke and shooting is all about. Just catch those girls and we'll take them with us."

He looked around the yard, the sudden carnage shocking even to him. "The boss sure isn't going to like this," he muttered to himself. Then he shrugged, "What the hell! Things don't always go the way he plans. Who would have thought Weston would be the one to stand up to us."

CHAPTER TWO

The two girls lay side by side on a bed in one of the second-floor bedrooms. The blue walls hung with pretty pictures, the white woodwork, the frilly canopy which arched over the bed all combined to make the blood splattered across the hand-embroidered bedspread even more horrible in contrast. The older girl still held the pistol she had used to kill first her sister then herself.

Every time a new man would enter the room he would stare for a moment at the scene and then try to find somewhere else to look. All of them had known and liked the two girls and there was a growing undercurrent of quiet anger in the room.

One of them, a worn, middle-aged man nervously crumpling his old hat in his hands, spoke, "This is just the way I found them, Sheriff. I saw they were dead and couldn't make myself stay in the room alone with them."

He cleared his throat noisily before he continued. "When me and Ezra got here after seeing the smoke from Franklin's barn, we found all that in the yard. Then Ezra noticed the girls wasn't down with the rest and we thought we best find them. Any men would do what they did out there would treat pretty girls like those real bad. Ezra looked through the outbuildings and I came in the house. I found them lying there, just like that." He sniffed loudly and had to look away. Ezra nodded in agreement.

A heavy-set man wearing a white doeskin jacket bent over the bodies and examined them carefully. Then he removed the revolver from the girl's hand and covered them with a blanket. This eased the tension in the room slightly. "You did right, Carl. I just wish either you or Ezra had seen the men who did this. Whoever has been doing this nightriding has gone too far this time."

Several of the men murmered in agreement. One demanded, "What are you going to do about this, Henry? This is going to make a lot of people real nervous, especially to the women. There have been too many people frightened out of this country already."

"What are you trying to say, Bill? That I'm not doing my job?" The Sheriff's face was pale, drained of all emotion.

"Some of us are beginning to wonder when you are going to put a stop to this, Henry." Bill's composure was shaken by the Sheriff's cold glare, but he was determined to make his point. "There have been seven families left this valley and never been seen or heard of again. Maybe they're all dead, like the Westons. Maybe this time the killers didn't have the time to get rid of the bodies."

A defensive look appeared on Sheriff Carr's face. "I know I should be doing more, Bill, but I just don't know what. The county has allowed me to take on some special deputies and they are on the move all the time, but it's almost as if the men who are doing this know just where I will be next."

"Are you sure you can trust all of those new deputies, Henry? Some of them look like pretty tough cases to me."

"It isn't any of them," Henry responded angrily. "You know the county can't afford to pay top wages. I have to make do with the men I can get. Up to now I have no reason to think any of them can't be trusted."

"Who else knows about your plans?" The speaker was a short, very thin man dressed in a dark, vested suit.

"I don't tell anyone, Bent. Even my deputies don't know where we are going in advance. I try not to set any patterns on when we go out, either, but they always seem to know." He looked around the room now uncomfortably full of men. "Maybe it is time there was a new Sheriff in this county. He might be able to find out what is going on. Fresh eyes might see something I've been missing."

"Don't do anything rash, Henry. You're doing as much as any man could. The rest of us just haven't been giving you the help you need. I think you should impose a curfew after dark. That way your deputies would know anyone they met is up to no good."

Bill shrugged. "That is a good idea for the future, Mr. Stiles. For now, hadn't we better see if we can get on the trail of the men who did this?"

The Sheriff groaned, "What trail? There isn't a track on the road leading away from here except for the ones Ezra made when he came to town for me. It looks like they used gunny sacks on their horses' hooves or something. There just isn't a mark out there to follow."

They stood in silence for another long spell. Finally the Sheriff coughed self-consciously and ordered, "A couple of you men carry these girls down to the yard. Clarence will be along any time for them."

He looked around the group. "Weston had a son back east somewhere, didn't he?"

Carl nodded. "Young Frank. Never met him, but his father was real proud of him. Going to one of those colleges in New England. Real smart boy, I guess. Franklin used to talk about him a good bit when we would get together."

Sheriff Carr stared at him in surprise, "You and

Weston used to get together? He was a rich man from the east. What would the two of you have in common?"

Carl spat on the polished floor and then tried to hide it with his boot. "Franklin was a farmer just like me and the rest. He never came on like no swell or," he paused meaningfully, "like no small town sheriff! He and his family was in my home several times and mine was in his. I think most of the men around here can say the same."

Several of them murmered in agreement. Ezra spoke up, "He was a good man, Henry. They were all good people. His oldest daughter, Mary—" he looked over at the lifeless lump under the blanket on the bed. "She stayed to my house for a couple of weeks last winter when my wife was down with the miseries. Did the cooking and the cleaning and looked after Mabel. My wife is going to be some broke up when she finds out she is dead."

"You catch these killers, Henry," Carl said bitterly. "We are supporting enough special deputies; you should have had these killers by now. Or you would have if these deputies got out of town once in a while and did some work instead of just drinking and gambling in to Sailor's Saloon."

Sheriff Carr turned on him. "You know that isn't true, Carl. They are out every night, looking. What more do you want?"

"I want you to catch the men did this, so our wives can sleep nights again," Carl answered pointedly.

"Gentlemen, gentlemen." Stiles raised his hands shoulder high, palms towards the angry group. "I'm sure Sheriff Carr is doing all he can."

"Up to now it ain't enough," muttered a voice at the back of the room.

A brooding silence fell, keeping the tension in the room high. Finally the Sheriff said, "Someone has to get word to his son."

"I will do that, Henry," Stiles offered, the change of subject taking some of the tension out of the air. "My wife grew up in the same town with the Weston's and the family of the girl young Frank is going to marry. She and Agnes Weston used to talk about it from time to time." The small man pulled a spotlessly white handkerchief from a pocket and blew his nose noisily. He then used a corner to wipe the moisture from his eyes before proceeding. "It might be better if the girl's parents broke the news to him rather than his getting it badly in a telegram. It will be hard enough for him as it is."

Sheriff Carr sighed in relief. "I appreciate your taking care of that, Bent. He used your bank, would you know if Franklin left a will? There might be someone else we should notify."

"He told me once he had made one out. I think Edgar has it on file in his office." The banker looked down at the floor. "I'm not sure there is as much money as people think, though. He owed the bank a good deal on the farm and he didn't have much cash in his current account. Oh, he was making enough to get by, but no great amounts of money. I think most of it went to keep his boy in college. From the way he talked, I think he may have moved out here so his friends back east wouldn't know how little he actually had left."

Sheriff Carr moved to the bed. "It doesn't matter much now. They're past worrying about things like that." He began to roll one of the girls in a blanket. "Let's get them downstairs."

"What happened? I told you no killings!"

"Weston was a tough man, Bent. He wasn't one to scare easy. Then when his kid came out with that shotgun, Jeff had no choice but to defend himself."

The two sat at a table in the backroom of the bank, a single lamp spreading a dim light across the surface between them. Carr was relaxed, chair tilted back on its rear legs, his boot heels hooked on the corner of the table. Stiles was more tense, hunched forward, weight resting on the table

The banker was angry. "We are going to have to call off the operation for a while. People around the county are really upset about the Westons. As long as it was just families leaving in the middle of the night or an occasional barn burnt, they worried, but they didn't panic." He rapped on the table with his fist for emphasis, "You will have to keep your men under better control in the future."

"Don't worry about my men. I'll handle them." The Sheriff's boots dropped to the floor. "Pay me the bonus money now so I can hand it over to the boys and then I'll keep them moving around for the next couple of weeks, make it look like they are hunting the killers. When nothing else happens they should get part of the credit."

Stiles pulled an envelope from a drawer in the

table and slid it across. "Another thing, Henry. You have got to start keeping your men quiet when they are in town. They do spend too much time over at Sailor's drinking and gambling. People have noticed. You heard those men out at Weston's this afternoon."

"What does it matter what people say? Another six months, a year at the most and we'll control the biggest part of the land we need. When that New York paper decides to go ahead with its model agricultural community, we will have the perfect location for them."

"That is just why it matters what people say. If that paper should hear the faintest suggestion of anything not being right, they won't touch this part of the state. They don't want the bad publicity they would get from their rival papers. Then we would be stuck with a lot of land we couldn't sell, couldn't even admit to owning. If the paper buys it no one will check to see who is selling because of the size of the transaction. They will just assume the bank acted as the agent for all those absent farmers. If we should try to sell individual farms, though..." His voice trailed off as the thought took hold.

"We still have the money from Weston's account. That must be a sizable sum itself."

Stiles snorted. "Just barely enough to keep your men happy. If we are going to make any real money out of this we have to play it smart." He held Carr's eyes motionless with the fervor in his small black ones. "Your men have killed now, don't let it happen again. They could start liking it and you might not be able to control them."

"Don't worry about me being able to control my men, Bent. They know better than to cross me. I've got enough stuff on them. A word in the proper place would get most of them hung."

"They would take you and me with them."

The Sheriff grinned smugly. "No one would believe them. Good old Henry Carr who dresses funny and pretends he is the marshal of a wild west cowtown? He wouldn't hurt a fly. All I would have to do is say I knew nothing about what was going on. Most people think I'm stupid enough they would believe me." He smiled broader. "On the other hand, Bent. They might believe it about you. You've never been one to go out of your way to make friends."

He sat forward, serious again. "Now how are we going to handle this kid of Weston's? I expect he will come out here to see the farm and collect his father's estate. He isn't going to believe there is no money."

"Leave that to me. By the time he gets here I will have all the paperwork necessary to prove my story. My wife says he is a bit of a selfish snob anyway. Doesn't like anything about the west. There is a good chance he will decide not to come out here at all, just send me instructions on how to settle his estate. Whatever he decides, I can handle it."

"I hope so," the Sheriff concluded.

CHAPTER THREE

The boy on the bicycle rode around the shoulder of the hill and down the long drive towards the house. Tonight his destination stood out from the other large houses in the exclusive neighborhood because of its brilliant illumination and the exuberant sounds of young people which could be heard for blocks in all directions.

The Johnstones were giving a party. The most important party of their daughter's young life. The one to celebrate her engagement. Their extensive two-story wooden house rambled along the side of the hill, its normal lighting augmented by strings of paper lanterns and gay decorations. They had spared no expense to make this a party the young couple would remember for the rest of their lives.

Their daughter was going to marry the son of the couple who were their best friends, people they hadn't seen for more than a year. They couldn't be present tonight and their absence threw the only damper on the party. The Westons had lived in the house next door for generations, the two families living almost as one. Both had been pleased when Emily and young Frank discovered a deeper interest in each other, one which had slowly matured until now they were ready to announce their engagement.

The wedding wouldn't take place until next spring after Frank had completed his studies at the university and was ready to enter the world of business. Though no longer active, his father still held large interests in the financial world and Frank's position would be secure. Of course, that would be after the extensive European tour Emily's parents were giving them for a wedding present.

The entire neighborhood had been invited along with the many friends of the two families and those of the happy couple. The french doors onto the wide porch were open giving the rooms a more spacious atmosphere and the party had spilled out onto the well lighted, and the less well lighted, parts of the lawn.

The young people were dancing to an excellent orchestra brought down from Boston for the occasion. The excitement of the evening was making it difficult for the servants to keep the huge punch bowl filled, even though it was being supplimented by a supply of harder beverages concealed in one of the outbuildings by several of the young gentlemen from the college.

The elders, who seemed to think their duties as chaperones to require only an occasional appearance, and that well advertised, had gathered in the library and the back parlor to allow the young the freedom to celebrate. It was a neighborhood with high standards of behavior, but with a good deal of common sense.

By eleven-fifteen when the boy on the bicycle arrived at the house the party had reached its peak and the noise level was deafening. He dismounted at the foot of the front steps and leaned on his two-wheeler against the mounting block before climbing the steps a little uncertainly to ring the bell.

While he stood waiting for some response a number of young people passed in and out, all ignoring him. He tried the bell again, this time twisting the handle vigorously which would normally have made the metallic clatter echo down the wide hall. Tonight he couldn't hear it above the noise. Deciding he would have to take more positive action if he were to deliver the telegram, he peered through the screen door.

A uniformed maid was carrying a tray loaded with clean glasses towards him down the hall from the pantry. He pulled the door open and pushed his way inside past a formally dressed youth. The young gentleman started to say something to him, but was distracted by catching sight of a girl he had been trying to meet all evening.

When the maid returned with an empty tray the boy grabbed her arm and waved the envelope under her nose, "I have a telegram for Mr. Johnstone. It's real important."

She reached out for it. "I'll take it to him."

"No," he said firmly. "I'm to give it to him personally."

She shrugged. "Suit yourself. I'll tell Mr. Speake."

The boy waited in the hall observing the party with interest until the butler, stiffly dressed in formal black, approached. "You may give me the telegram, young man," he said officiously.

The boy looked him up and down. "You ain't Mr. Johnstone. I've been out here before."

"He is busy at the moment and doesn't wish to come to the door. He instructed me to accept it for him."

"The office told me to only give it to Mr. Johnstone personal. I ain't about to give it to no one else."

The man sighed deeply. "Follow me then."

He led the boy down the hall to a massive set of double doors which he opened, gesturing for the boy to wait in the hall. He bent over a man sitting at a card table in the hot, crowded room and whispered in his ear. The man directed an exasperated look at the door and the boy recognized Mr. Johnstone. The butler straightened and beckoned to him and he crossed the room to stand in discomfort beside the table until the hand was completed.

Mr. Johnstone played his last card, watched his opponent add the trick to the long string already in front of him and muttered to the boy with exasperation. "I suppose this is another wire of congratulations. I don't know why you couldn't have given it to John."

"I was told to give it to you personal, sir. That it was important."

"Give it here then."

The boy handed it over and watched with interest as it was torn open. Mr. Johnstone read it through hurriedly and then, with a shocked expression, again more slowly. He glanced around the room, seemingly unsure what to do.

He found the boy waiting and said, "John. Give him five dollars. He followed orders and there was a good reason for them. We haven't been very pleasant to him and I want him to have a reward for sticking to his guns."

The boy followed the butler out of the room, pleased and surprised with the tip which was more than double his week's wages.

William Johnstone sat for a time in thought and then stood slowly, explaining to his curious partners, "Please continue your game. This is a business matter I have to take care of immediately." The others were troubled by his behavior, but his manner did not invite questions.

He crossed the crowded room to where his wife was listening to their minister talk about the problems the war in Europe caused for travelers and managed to extract her from the man's clutches without arousing his curiosity.

As he led her upstairs his expression prevented her from asking questions. The only privacy he could find was in her cluttered sewing room.

He shut the door firmly behind them and turned to face her. "Please sit down, Elizabeth. I have just received some terrible news and I'm not quite sure what to do." He urged her towards the seat in the bay window overlooking the celebration in the front yard.

"What is it, Will?" Her voice mirrored her growing concern.

He sat beside her, his mind ignoring the gaity on the well lighted lawn below. "It is the Westons in Colorado," he began. "I'm afraid they've been killed."

"Oh, Will! How terrible." She reached out a hand to him. "Was it some kind of accident?"

He shook his head violently. "They were murdered, Liz. Some kind of gang killed them all, right in their own home!" He handed her the telegram.

She extracted the spectacles she had to use for reading from a hidden recess in her dress and carefully studied the message. Then she looked up at him, her emotions back under control. "We have to tell Frank, Will. It isn't something we can put off."

"Couldn't we let him finish the party before we tell him? It might be the last happiness he will know for some time."

"He has to be told now, Will. There are decisions

he will have to make and they can't be put off." She cleared her throat. "You know as well as I do he isn't a strong-willed boy, and Emily is not yet ready to provide the strength he needs. Neither one is mature enough yet to accept the responsibility for dealing with this properly. You and I will have to see they make the right decisions." She laid a comforting hand on his arm. "I know this is hard for you, dear, but we have to think of Frank and Emily and their future. I'll go down and get him. I think you should break it to him alone. It will be easier for you both."

Will nodded gloomily. "Give me a few minutes to decide how to do it."

Elizabeth managed to remove Frank from the party without much fuss. Emily was dancing with one of Frank's friends and she didn't disturb her. She gave him the impression Will wanted to talk to him about a family matter, so he wasn't very concerned when he arrived in the sewing room.

Will apologized for the meeting place while Elizabeth was withdrawing. "It was the only room left in the entire house where we could be alone and I have to talk to you in private, Frank."

The boy was a bit surprised by the gloomy manner of his future father-in-law, but he managed to conceal it as he said politely, "It doesn't matter, sir. What did you want to see me about?"

Will abruptly handed him the telegram. "Bad news about your family, I'm afraid. This arrived a few minutes ago. It will tell you all I know." He coughed self-consciously.

Frank read the message slowly, his hands beginning to shake as he comprehended what it said. He folded the sheet of paper with nervous fingers and stared unseeingly at a dress form across the room for several minutes. Finally he said in a confused voice, "I don't see how it is possible."

"I can only assume it was the work of one of those bands of killers we read about in the paper. Your father wouldn't have done anything to provoke them and your mother never had an unkind word for anyone. Elizabeth and I are heartbroken about this." He wanted to put his arm around the boy's shoulders, but suddenly realized he couldn't. "We want to do whatever we can to help. I want you to consider our home your home from now on."

Frank didn't appear to have heard him as he sat and stared at the telegram his fingers continued to fold into smaller and smaller rectangles. When he looked up again his eyes were moist, but his voice was controlled, though faint. "Do I have to go out there?"

Will was surprised by the question. "What do you mean?"

"Do I have to go out to this miserable little town in Colorado?" Frank was calm, eyes steady on Will's face.

"Someone will have to see your family is properly taken care of. You would be the one people would expect to go."

"I don't see why. I'm sure you can find someone to go out there in my place. Someone who is used to that sort of thing."

William Johnstone stood stiffly, one hand grasping one of the knobs at the top of a ladderback chair, the other clenched into a fist behind his back. "Don't you want to know what happened to your family, Frank? Know that these killers have been brought to justice? You are the last of the Weston family, Frank. You owe it to your dead!" He had trouble keeping the anger from his voice.

Frank shrugged, his normal languid manner again apparent. "I don't see why. They are dead. My going all the way out there won't bring them back. Besides," he said casually as he flicked at a piece of lint on his lapel with the folded telegram," Ferdie Potts has asked me to crew for him this summer. If I go out west I will have to give that up."

A more observant person than Frank might have noticed the tightening of Will Johnstone's lips or the whiteness of the knuckles of the hand which gripped the chair knob and at least attempted to hide his indifference. Unfortunately, Frank didn't.

Will had to force himself to relax his grip on the knob. "Please excuse me," he said in a strained voice. "I want to have a word with my wife before we continue." To Frank's amazement he lurched unsteadily across the room, jerked open the door, stepped into the hall and closed it firmly behind himself.

Elizabeth had been waiting in the hall to be certain they wouldn't be disturbed. She put a hand on his arm in concern. "Good heavens, Will. What happened?"

"He says he can't go out to settle his father's affairs because Ferdie Potts has asked him to go sailing this summer and it would interfere. He wants me to find a suitable substitute."

"I see," she said calmly, patting his arm. "You know Frank has trouble making decisions, Will. What he needs is the proper incentive. You wait here and I'll handle this."

He held the door open and she walked across the room to sit beside Frank in the window. "Will has told me, Frank. I'm sure your father would be very proud."

Frank gaped at her, not sure of her meaning.

"Of course it is the only thing people of our class could do in a situation such as this. When it is a personal or family matter only a member of that family can properly handle it. I am so pleased you recognize that and have decided to act as a gentleman should. We all are so impressed."

She sat and looked him directly in the eye. "You do realize, of course, if you had come to any other decision Emily would have had to call off the engagement. She has very high standards as to what is proper. After all, there are things one does when he is of our class."

He stared at her for a long moment before finally dropping his eyes. "You're right, of coure," he whispered. "It is the only thing I could do."

"You are being very wise, Frank. I'm sure you will be happy with your decision." She went to the door and brought her husband back inside. "Frank has decided he should be the one to go to Colorado."

Will was a bit dubious about this sudden change of heart, but he was not about to ask his wife how it

33

had been accomplished. His manner was still a little distant when he stated, "I am pleased to hear it, Frank."

There was a short, heavy silence while Frank adjusted to his new line of thinking. He finally changed the subject to a neutral ground. "Why was my family killed? It doesn't make any sense to me."

Will indicated the telegram. "You read what this man Stiles said. They don't know why or even who did it. I am sure he would have told us more if there had been more to tell."

"I'm sure you are right, sir. It's just..." He looked at the telegram and then across to Elizabeth. "I suppose I do have to know exactly what happened and who did it before I can do anything else with my life. If I had been killed, father would have made sure the people who did it were punished. I don't suppose I can do any less for him."

She nodded encouragingly and the boy began to relax slightly. The thought of losing Emily and his place with the Johnstones had frightened him badly.

Will wondered for a moment if Elizabeth might not have gone too far. "You will have to be careful out there, Frank. You don't know what kind of people these are. Any community where an entire family could be wiped out and not leave a clue can't be a very safe place. You might be in danger yourself."

"It is something I have to do, sir, if I am to live the kind of life I want." He was working hard to convince himself of the idea.

Elizabeth smiled at him warmly for the first time.

"He will be all right, Will. Why don't you go down and bring up Emily. We have some family decisions to make and he should be present. You might also have John come up and stand watch in the hall. We don't want to be interrupted by any of the guests."

She waited in the open door until John arrived and then went back inside with Frank. "We have to decide just how you are going to make this trip, dear," she stated as she sat beside him. "We also must tell Emily."

The door opened again and a pretty girl of eighteen entered just in time to hear the last sentence. She was obviously making a strong effort to control her emotions. "Emily knows. Daddy told me on the way up." She crossed to sit beside Frank, taking his hand in both of her's. "I am so proud of you, darling. Going all the way out there to make sure justice is done for your family." For a moment it appeared her control wouldn't be enough and the tears would slip out, but she supressed them.

If Frank had had any doubts about the right course of action they were gone now. Her father had waited in the doorway, John looking over his shoulder. Elizabeth broke the spell when she said, "Close the door, dear. We have plans to make."

They settled in a group beside the window and she continued, "First we have to get Frank out of here and on his way west. I'm sure you can handle the arrangements, Will. Emily and I will make sure he is properly packed."

"What about the party?" her daughter asked.

"That can continue without us for the time being.

What Frank doesn't need is the morbid curiosity and false sympathy he would have to endure if they found out We want to have him well on his way before we tell them."

Emily held Frank's hand to her cheek for a moment. "You go along to your room and start packing your things. The last train to New York leaves in about an hour. I want to ride that far with you."

After the two had left she turned to her mother. "I want to go to Colorado, Mother. He is such an innocent about some things. They could hurt him badly. I don't think I should travel with him because he might think I don't trust him, but I want to be there if he should need me." She thought a moment, "Don't you have an old friend from your school days in this Singleshoe?"

Elizabeth held her daugher tightly for a moment, more pleased than she would say. For some time now she had been worried about the obvious weaknesses in Frank's character and thought her daughter was blind to them. Now that she knew the girl recognized and accepted them, the worry she had been carrying about their marriage diminished. "I do know someone there. Matilda Stiles. Her husband owns the bank. He sent us the telegram about Frank's family. I'm sure she would be delighted to have you stay with her. She has a daughter she wants to get into Laurel Heights and I can be a help to her."

She held her daughter close for a moment longer. "I understand why you have to do this, baby. I think

36

I would do the same if it were your father. Don't worry about things here, I will take care of them."

Suddenly business-like and organized, she said, "You have already told Frank you want to ride as far as New York with him. You can stay with cousin Alice while you are there. I will pack what you need for the trip and see that enough money is sent to cover your expenses. You can take the train the day after Frank."

A thought occured to her. "No. I think three days later might be better. You don't want to chance catching up with him if he happens to miss a connection. The worst thing which could happen at a time like this would be for him to think you don't trust him out there alone. He might never forgive you."

Emily agreed. "It should also give you time to arrange things with Mrs. Stiles."

Her composure suddenly faltered and she began to cry. "It just doesn't seem possible it could have happened. Mary and Ruth were my best friends ever. None of that family ever harmed a living thing."

Elizabeth pulled her close again while the tears she had held back for Frank's sake spilled out. "Get it all out, baby. You are going to have to be the strength Frank doesn't have. You can't let him see you break down, ever. He will have enough problems to contend with in that country of barbarians without that."

The sobs slowly died away and Emily wiped her eyes and face with her handkerchief. "I'm all right now," she sniffed. Then she blew her nose in a very unladylike manner.

Elizabeth had been strengthened by her daughter's tears and now began to consider what else had to be done. "We should telegraph Katherine. I don't think they would know about her in Singleshoe, and she should be told of Franklin's death."

"I thought no one around here knew where she was, or didn't want to know."

"Her reputation may not be of the best, Emily, but I always liked her. We write now and then, so I do know how to reach her. I believe Franklin always kept in touch with her, also. He felt she should do what she wanted and not to worry what the rest of us though. If we can find her, she would be a big help to you and Frank."

CHAPTER FOUR

"Are you telling me you have no idea who murdered my family?" Frank sat stiffly on the front six inches of a straight-backed chair, his voice coldly formal as he glowered at the sheriff.

It was difficult for him to believe the caricature sitting across from him was really the Sheriff of Singleshoe. The man looked like a drawing in a cheap western magazine. His sizeable stomach hung well out over the belt of his tailored pants. His shirt was a work of art, decorated with bead work and embroidery, topped with a black string tie held closed at the neck by a huge piece of silver-mounted turquoise. The costume was completed by a white doeskin jacket with long leather fringe. Henry Carr would have been perfect as the ringmaster for a second-rate wild west show, but Frank refused to take him seriously as the county sheriff.

The man's superior manner was also difficult for him to accept as he lectured, "You have to realize, Mr. Weston, that things are not the same out here as they are back east. These were men who knew how to hide their trail. I don't even know which way they turned after they went out the gate. Any tracks they might have left had been completely eliminated before I arrived. I just don't know who they were or where they went."

"Surely it is not possible for that many men to ride very far in broad daylight without someone observing them. Have you bothered to ask?" Frank's tone left no doubt as to his lack of confidence.

"Of course I've asked!" Sheriff Carr growled. "I've been over this whole part of the country asking. It just happens that west of your father's place is some very rough country, not a house for miles. If they went in there I wouldn't have a chance of finding them. Since I can't find a trace of them anywhere else, that must be just where they've gone."

"Then all you have to do is gather your men together and go in there and look, isn't it?" Frank asked primly.

Carr took several moments to regain control before he replied, "You listen to me real careful, boy. I'm going to explain it to you just one more time. That is some of the worst cut-up country you ever saw. There is no way of finding anyone in there who doesn't want to be found. The chances of my taking a posse in there and bringing them back are almost none. There are just too many places for them to set an ambush."

"Could it be that you are afraid to do your duty, Sheriff?" Frank demanded with contempt.

Henry Carr was suddenly on his feet, leaning forward across the desk, weight resting on his hands. His face flushed bright red and his voice grated as he growled, "What the hell do you mean talking to me like that? A young pup like you fresh to the west. If I hadn't liked your father, who was always a gentleman I might add, I'd take you out behind the barn and beat you senseless for saying that to me."

For the first time Frank's air of superiority faltered. He sat back in the chair and stared open-mouthed at the enraged man looming above him.

"Your parents were damn good people," Carr continued angrily. "I knew them both well and I intend to find the men who killed them. Not because some stuffed-up whippersnapper with a smart mouth tells me it is my duty, but because I do my job damn well."

Frank finally found his voice. "I'm sure I didn't mean..."

The Sheriff wouldn't let him finish. "Benton Stiles over at the bank is expecting you. Why don't you go over there and let me get on with my work."

"Really, Sheriff. There is no reason for you to react in this manner. I'm sure I didn't mean to upset you." Frank found his elbow grasped firmly by a huge hand and himself propelled through the door and onto the sidewalk. The door slammed violently behind him, shaking dust down from the wooden awning above.

He turned to look back at the heavy door and shrugged his rumpled coat back into place. The violent reaction of the Sheriff had come as a shock to him. Back home no policeman would have dared to address him in that manner, let alone lay a hand on him and throw him out of his office. They expected their betters to tell them how to do their job.

The people in this barren part of the west seemed to think everyone was equal. Why his parents had wanted to come out here to live when they had a perfectly respectable home in the east with decent people around who knew their place was beyond him. And their letters had seemed to indicate they liked it here. It just didn't seem possible.

The bank was a block east and on the other side of the street. Its heavy brick construction made it the only substantial structure in the town. He stepped from the walk to the street and directly into the path of an approaching rider. The man swore violently at him as he reined his horse to one side, using words which had not been directed towards Frank before in his entire life.

A subdued and very confused young man continued on to the bank. This certainly was a very different country from that to which he was accustomed. The people here just didn't seem to know their place.

The dim, cool interior of the bank somewhat

restored his confidence. The three teller's windows with the heavy door of the safe standing open behind them gave a feeling of substantial security. He paused for a moment just inside the door to breath the cool air and compose himself. Then he walked across to the area enclosed by a low railing which fronted the door marked: BENTON STILES, PRESIDENT.

The door opened and a tall, gaunt man of indeterminant age asked primly, "May I help you?"

"My name is Frank Weston. I believe Mr. Stiles is expecting me."

He looked him up and down, seemingly impressed by his appearance. This time when he spoke it was with more respect. "Mr. Stiles is expecting you, Mr. Weston, but he has someone with him at the moment. We didn't know exactly when you would be finished at the Sheriff's office." He indicated one of the chairs inside the railing. "Won't you have a seat while you wait?" He then sat behind the desk inside the railing and Frank watched him copy several letters into a large book.

The door finally opened again and a big man in faded bib overalls was ushered out by a short, thin man, impeccably dressed in a dark grey vested suit. The heavy gold chain which hung from watch to fob pocket across his stomach swung slightly as he moved. The man exhuded an aura of command and respectability, the perfect picture of a man you could trust with your money.

He was shaking the big man's hand as the other said, "Thanks for the help, Mr. Stiles. You won't regret taking a chance on me."

"If I thought I would regret it, Samson, I wouldn't have risked the bank's money. You have proven your ability. I think you should have the opportunity to profit from it." He held the gate in the railing open for the man to depart and turned to contemplate Frank expectantly with tiny black eyes which seemed to look right inside him.

The secretary said, "This is Frank Weston, Mr. Stiles."

"Of course it is," he said heartily. "I should have recognized him at once. I've seen his picture often enough in his parent's parlor." The smile faded suddenly. "I do apologize for that, Frank. I still have trouble realizing they are gone. You have my deepest sympathy."

Frank shifted uncomfortably under the cold, black eyes. "Thank you , sir. I also want to thank you for making the arrangements for their funeral."

"It was the least my wife and I could do, Frank. We thought a lot of your family. I'm only sorry we couldn't wait for your arrival."

"I understand about that, sir."

The banker noticed the avid attention his secretary was devoting to the conversation. "Come into my office, Frank. It will be more private there."

When he had Frank seated in a comfortable leather chair and had occupied the one behind his large desk, he said, "I hope the trip wasn't too difficult. Our trains are not very comfortable, I'm afraid."

"It was hot and dirty, but that is not important.

What is important is my making sure the men who killed my family are found and punished." His expression changed. "I'm not at all sure the Sheriff shares that interest."

"Good heavens! Whatever gave you that impression?" The banker's surprise was obvious.

"When I arrived at his office this morning I found him asleep behind his desk. His clothing was so neat I doubt he had done anything active in days."

"Don't underestimate our sheriff," the banker warned. "He had been out day and night looking for the men who murdered your family. I sent him word you were arriving today and would probably want to talk with him. He came in early this morning especially for that purpose. I would think he is probably exhausted."

"Well, that wasn't all. He made excuses for not finding the killers and they weren't very good."

"What kind of excuses?"

"Something about rough country where no one lives west of my father's farm. He said he wouldn't be able to find anyone in there and wasn't going to go in and look. I think he was afraid.'

"I certainly hope you didn't tell him that!"

"As a matter of fact, I did, and he threw me out of his office. His manners are not very good."

"His manners!" Stiles coughed once and then blew his nose in a large white handkerchief. "Frank. I hope you won't mind my talking to you like your father would have in this instance. You are a very lucky young man. Henry Carr is not a man you accuse of cowardice. You are fortunate he didn't beat you half to death, or worse."

"He did threaten to do it." Frank was a little surprised at the banker's attitude. He had expected better of him.

"Henry liked your father, so he must have taken that into account. You must be careful what you say to people out here, Frank. Never call a man a coward. He will have to prove he isn't by fighting you."

"That hardly seems civilized."

"You must remember we are a new part of the country. We get very touchy about our rights." He stood and walked to a cabinet. "Would you like a drink?"

"No, thank you, sir. I don't drink hard liquor this early in this afternoon." His tone was disapproving.

The banker sighed deeply and poured himself a stiff drink which he downed in one swallow before returning to his desk. He looked Frank directly in the eye as he said, "You leave those killers to Henry Carr. He will find them and we will hang them. Henry is a good man and works hard at his job. Please try to remember it is not like the settled east out here. Sometimes we have to do things a little differently."

"If you say so, sir," Frank agreed reluctantly. "I suppose I was a bit rough on him. Do you think I should go back and apologize for my behavior?"

"It wouldn't hurt, Frank. It might make Henry feel a little better about you." He shuffled some papers in a folder on his desk. "When do you plan to return east?"

"Not until the killers of my family have met justice. I have to see it done."

Stiles was a bit surprised. "That could take some time."

"I have nothing else to do that is as important." Frank's voice was very determined. "May we talk about my father's estate? I would like to get all that settled as quickly as possible."

The banker shifted uncomfortably. "I'm afraid things are not exactly as you might expect."

"Do you mean he didn't leave a will? Even if he didn't, I am his only close relative, so there should be no problem."

"He did leave a will, Frank. It mentions you and his sister, Katherine Stone."

Frank flushed slightly, "I am surprised at that. We didn't mention her around home. Most people felt she led too free a life."

"Your father thought enough of her to name her executrix of his will if your mother died before him."

"That is strange. I didn't even know they communicated. Does that mean we won't be able to settle it now?"

"I'm afraid we will have to wait until she is present. There has been some problem in locating her. Perhaps you know where she is?"

Frank shook his head.

Stiles cleared his throat nervously. "I don't suppose it really makes much difference. You might as well know now there isn't much to settle."

"I don't understand. My father was a well-off man."

"Your father made some mistakes over the past year, I'm afraid. He used his money very unwisely."

Frank stared at him, unable to understand. "He never mentioned any money problems in his letters. How could he lose that much? He was very experienced when it came to financial matters."

Benton Stiles looked at him with sympathy. "Your father was too good a man, Frank. When one of his neighbors would come to me for a loan and couldn't meet our requirements I would have to turn them down. Your father would then lend him the money. Sometimes people took advantage of his friendship. Several times over the past year he had loaned people large sums of money only to have them leave the country soon after with no trace of where they had gone. I tried to warn him of the risk he was taking, but he wasn't the type of man to hear anything bad about his friends."

"That does sound like him," Frank sat very still as he asked, "Just how much is left?"

"Almost nothing, I'm afraid." Stiles shifted uncomfortably in his chair. "His ready cash was gone some time ago and he had to mortgage his farm for equipment for the spring planting. He would probably have worked it out if he had lived, but he didn't. I have no choice but to take over the farm. This is not a large enough bank that we can afford to let the debt go uncollected. I'm sure you can understand my position."

Frank nodded dumbly. He did understand. After all, he intended to go into banking himself. One couldn't be a success and let personal feelings enter

48

into it.

"Then there is nothing left at all?"

"Just the furnishings in the house. I'm sure we will be able to get you something for them once your aunt arrives and we can hold a sale."

The banker came around the desk and put his hand on the boy's shoulder. "My wife and I would like you to come stay with us while you are in Singleshoe. I know all this has been a great shock and you should be among friends."

Frank considered it and then shook his head. "No. Thank you for the offer, but I have enough money of my own. I don't want to impose on you and Mrs. Stiles. I will stay at the hotel as long as I am here." He was staring at his hands and didn't see the look of relief on Stiles' face.

The banker returned to his chair. "Now you see why I think it would be best for you to return east. This is no country for you. Go back and start a life of your own. I understand from my wife you have just become engaged."

"Yes," Frank said absently. "I have to think about all of this. It isn't a decision I can make quickly."

Stiles escorted him to the gate in the railing. "There is no hurry, Frank. And remember, if you ever need anything, I'm always available."

He watched the boy leave the bank and turn towards the hotel. Taking his hat from the rack in his office he said to his secretary. "I'll be at the Sheriff's office if anyone wants me."

CHAPTER FIVE

Henry Carr poured each of them a shot of whiskey from the bottle he kept in his desk drawer before
he asked, "How did he take it?"

"He seems to accept it," Stiles answered. "I think
it was the emphasis on how good a man his father
was and on how his friends had taken advantage of
him. Fit right in with his opinion of Singleshoe, I
believe. Of you especially. He doesn't think you
have any manners."

The Sheriff chuckled. "I got that impression.

How long do you figure he will stay around town?"

"A couple of days at the most. What can he do? He doesn't know how to get in touch with his aunt who is to handle the estate. I had been worried about her, but it turns out she is kind of the black sheep of the family." He finished his drink. "If you stay out of town so he thinks you are hunting the killers for the next few days I think he will go back east and leave it all in our hands."

"That'll be no problem. There's a stream over west I've been wanting to fish for some time. I won't come back until he's gone."

Stiles nodded. "That should just about do it. As long as nothing happens to change his attitude we are on our way to a lot of money."

He raised the refilled glass in a toast to the Sheriff.

Frank went for a long walk after registering at the hotel, trying to work out in his troubled mind just what he should do. He didn't see how Emily or her parents could expect him to do more than he had. There was really no reason for him to stay on in Singleshoe. Nothing further could be done without Aunt Katherine and no one knew where she was.

Hot and thirsty from his walk he paused in front of a saloon a couple of blocks up the street from the hotel. Its dim interior was inviting and curiosity made him push through the bat-wing doors.

The long, narrow room had a bar down the left side and a scattering of tables across the remaining space. In the back was a single poker table, the lamp

51

suspended above it throwing a bright circle of light across the five men seated around it.

One man leaned nonchalantly on the end of the bar watching the game and a bartender at the front was reading a newspaper by the light filtering through the flyspecked front window. He walked across to the bar and laid his derby on the top. The bartender looked up from his paper and asked, "What'll it be, Mac?"

"Do you have any cold beer?"

The man climbed down from the stool on which he had been perched, twitched his dirty apron straight and picked up one of the glass mugs standing mouth down on a clean towel. He filled it from the spout and set it in front of Frank, waiting patiently until a silver dollar was placed on the bar in payment. He made change from a box under the bar and said, "You want anything else, just holler."

Frank nodded indifferently in response and contemplated the sparse foam at the top of the mug. The beer was warm and flat.

"Hey, Sailor." a man called from the poker table. "Let's have a fresh bottle back here."

The bartender picked a full bottle from a shelf on the back bar and walked to the rear of the room. Not really interested in the warm beer, Frank's eyes followed him.

He straightened suddenly.

The men at the table were wearing stars pinned to their shirts or vests.

When the bartender returned Frank asked, "Who are those men? They all seem to be wearing badges of some kind."

Sailor shrugged. "Sheriff's deputies. Taken on to stop all this trouble's been going on out in the valley."

Frank turned to look at the noisy group again. "They just get in?"

Sailor had returned to his newspaper. His answer was muffled. "Nope. Been hanging around in here most of a week now. Haven't done much except get drunk and gamble. Guess there ain't any work for them right now. Things been pretty quiet since that farmer and his family were killed."

Frank took a deep drink of the tasteless beer then walked slowly down the room until he stood behind one of the poker players. A couple of the men looked up, decided he wasn't going to join the game, then ignored him. The man behind whom he was standing, directed an irritated look over his shoulder and Frank moved to one side.

He stood for several minutes watching the relaxed play, listening to the banter among the players and growing more and more angry. It was obvious the men had no intentions of breaking up this game any time soon and going out to hunt for the killers of his family. Now he knew he couldn't quit and go home. If he did the Sheriff would probably sit in his office and these men drink and gamble and no one would catch the murderers.

Unable to control his anger any longer, he slammed a hand down in the midst of the pile of cards the dealer was gathering. "Stop it!" he yelled.

They all stared at him in surprise.

"Why are you just sitting here?" he demanded. "You should be out looking for them men killed my family."

The man leaning on the end of the bar asked, "Who are you, kid?"

"I am Frank Weston. I demand you get out and find those killers!"

He grabbed the edge of the table and, with a violent jerk, scattered the money and cards across the floor as he overturned it. "Why don't you do what you are being paid to do?" His voice had risen until it was almost a shriek.

One of the men looked up at him, a smile growing on his face. "All right, Weston. You want it, I'm the man can give it to you." He and the others rose and surrounded Frank.

"Not in here, boys. You want to do any fighting, take him outside." The bartender had come down the bar holding a scattergun.

"Whatever you say, Sailor, but I'm holding you responsible for our money while we're gone." The speaker grasped Frank by the lapels of his suit and hurled him roughly towards a door in the back wall.

Frank tried to resist. "You can't do this to me. You are officers of the law." A tight knot of fear was growing in his stomach as he read the look in the faces of the men.

They laughed as he staggered through the back door, lost his footing and fell heavily in the midst of a pile of empty bottles. "You hear that, Jeff?" the first speaker asked. "We can't do this to him. We're lawmen."

Jeff grabbed Frank by the belt and dragged him from the pile. "Stand up, little man. Take what you got coming."

Frank jerked free and spun to one side. A man standing ready drove a left into the pit of his stomach. He sagged over as his breath whoosed out and someone else booted him hard in the rear. The first two blows ignited a pain in his body which grew as the men pushed and pulled, turning him into this blow, throwing him at that one. They concentrated on his body, not wanting to mark his face.

They stopped at last from pure exhaustion. Jeff held him erect and breathed a vile whiskey breath directly into his face from only a couple of inches away. "Can you hear me, boy?"

Frank managed to nod, though in truth he could barely make out what the man was saying. The aches and pains from the blows seemed to have set his body on fire.

"This is just a sample of what you'll get," Jeff promised ominously, "If you stay around Single-shoe. I think you would be smart to get as far from here as you can. Maybe go clear back east where you came from. Don't you think that is a good idea?"

A blast from a shotgun shattered the pile of bottles beside them into a mass of flying fragments. "Nobody moves!" commanded a powerful voice.

"Can you walk, Weston?" it asked. "If so, get clear of them."

Frank shuffled slowly to one side, both arms wrapped around his aching stomach, and leaned up against the back wall of an outhouse across the alley:

"Now turn around real careful," the voice ordered the deputies. "I would be delighted if any of you would be foolish enough to do something stupid so I can shoot the lot of you."

"This is no concern of yours, Karren. You don't want to mix in where you don't belong." Jeff's voice was dangerous.

The man wasn't impressed. "You scum drop your gunbelts." They did as he ordered and stepped back out of reach.

"Now you all go back inside Sailor's. You can come out after we're gone and fetch your guns." He chuckled softly. "I would like it a lot if you were to come back while I was still around. This town would be the better for a few less of your kind."

They followed his instructions, sulking badly. When they were inside Karren wedged a length of two by four against the door and turned to Frank.

As he assisted him down the alley he said, "You should be a bit more careful who you associate with." He opened the back door to a large frame structure at the end of the next block. "I'll get you to a bed and send for the Doc." He locked the door carefully behind them.

Frank was growing curious despite his pain as they shuffled down a dark hall. "Where are we?"

"The hotel. I'll put you in my room. Neither Carr nor his men are quite ready to tangle with me just yet, so you should be safe there. As soon as you can travel I'll send you down to talk to the one man who can help us find out what is going on around here."

Frank held back for a moement. "Why are you helping me? It could get you in a lot of trouble."

Will Karren grinned selfconsciously. "Selfishness. As long as people are afraid they don't come to town and sleep in my beds or eat in my dining room. I want the town back the way it was."

The boy shook his head. "I think it is more than that."

"I live in this town. It's my home," Will admitted, finally. "A man fights to keep his home free."

As Will let him down upon the bed Frank asked, "Then why do we need this other man?"

"Because he is a gunfighter. He can stand up to men like Carr and his deputies. We have to have someone who knows what he is doing." Karren looked Frank right in the eye, "And we have to have someone who knows how to kill!"

CHAPTER SIX

"I don't like her coming here, Matilda. Having a stranger in my home makes me uncomfortable. What does she want out here anyway?"

"She is engaged to young Frank Weston and is worried about him. I think it is very brave of her to come all this way to be near him."

Benton Stiles irritably paced up and down in front of the bench on which his wife calmly sat knitting. It was still ten minutes before the train was due and the depot waiting room was empty, other than themselves. "Why does she have to stay with us, Mat? I don't want to be responsible for a girl that age."

"I've known her mother for years, Benton. Who else would she stay with while she is here? When

May goes back to Laurel Heights to start school the year after next, Elizabeth has agreed to keep an eye on her. We can't very well send her otherwise, and I do want May to go to the same school I did." She looked up at her husband, the needles quiet in her hands. "If we had refused to take Emily then there would be no way I could have asked Elizabeth to take May. That is the way it is, Benton." Her head bent and the needles resumed their clicking.

The banker knew he had little chance of changing his wife's mind once it was made up. The Weston boy had left town, anyway. Perhaps it wouldn't matter.

"Did you tell Frank that Emily was arriving today?"

He looked down at her in surprise. "Why should I?"

"Because I asked you to yesterday." There was a trace of exasperation in her voice. "Did you see him at all?"

"I couldn't find him. It seems he had gone south for some reason or other."

Her needles stopped again. "He will be back, won't he? We have to be able to tell Emily all about him."

"I don't know his plans, dear. I haven't seen him since the day he came to my office."

She stared at him for a long moment, her eyes seeming to look deep inside him. "You will tell her he is just gone for a few days. That he will be back soon."

It was an order and he ruffled under it. "Why

should I? If she thinks he won't be coming back, perhaps she will go back home where she belongs."

"I don't want her to go home too soon, Benton. She has to stay with us long enough and be treated well enough to put her mother under a strong obligation to me. I want Elizabeth to feel it is her duty to look after May."

Stiles sighed in exasperation. "I don't see why it is so blasted important for her to go back to that school just because you went there. A number of schools here in the west are just as good."

Her eyes were cold. "My daughter won't be marrying any of these out-of-pocket ranchers and settling down to having child after child until she is worn out at thirty. I want her to have the chance to marry as well as possible. It is the least we can do to ensure her future happiness." Her voice was bitter and her husband knew better than to reopen that argument again.

The banker was saved by the arrival of the train from the east. His wife calmly packed her knitting away in a large bag and stood, smoothing her dress into place. She marched across the wide platform and took up a position at the foot of the steps of the Pullman car. The men whose duties required their presence at the train tipped their hats respectfully as they passed. They tried to avoid Benton. The story of the beating of the Weston boy by the deputies was all over town and a lot of people were holding him responsible. Damn that Karren, anyway, Benton thought. Why couldn't he mind his own business?

The porter placed the wooden step at the foot of

the stairs leading to the rear platform of the through Pullman. The first person to step into view was a woman, tall and beautifully proportioned, her reddish-brown hair fastened in a tight bun at the nape of her neck. Benton observed her descent of the steps with admiration. She obviously wore no stiff undergarments which would restrain the motion of her fine body. Her eyes swept across him and he was surprised to discover the controlled emotion behind them. He was also surprised to discover she must be in her mid-thirties. At first glance he had taken her to be in her early twenties. The porter handed her a small carpetbag and she moved off towards the baggage car, Benton's eyes following her every move.

"There she is." His wife's pleased cry brought his attention back to the platform. Another pretty girl, this one with her dark hair floating free in a well brushed cascade down her back, stood at the top of the steps. She was the type of pretty girl who could grow beautiful as she got older. Matilda waved excitedly at her and she smiled tentatively in return.

She descended the steps to be engulfed in one of Matilda's matronly hugs. It was apparent she was tired and a bit mussed from the long trip, but alert and curious about her surroundings.

"I hope the trip wasn't too bad, Emily, dear." His wife mothered, brushing at the soot on the girl's shoulders. Even the well constructed Pullman couldn't keep the grit of the locomotive away from a traveler.

"I enjoyed it," she responded. "It is all so big and

empty out here, isn't it?" She looked around. "Where's Frank? Did you tell him I was coming?"

"We didn't have the chance, dear. He went south for a few days just before we received your mother's wire. How is Elizabeth, by the way? I hear so little from back home these days."

"Mother? She's fine." She accepted Benton's proffered arm and they walked through the depot to the waiting buggy. "How is Frank bearing up under all this? It must be very hard on him."

Benton patted her arm. "He is doing just fine, my dear. It shows the fine stock from which he comes." She was taller than he and when she looked down on him it made him just a bit self-conscious.

"I'm glad you weren't able to tell him I was coming. I would rather he didn't know I was here for the time being. He might think I didn't trust him out here alone."

"We won't tell, dear," Matilada assured her. "At least not until you want us to. Men do like to think they can get along without us, don't they?"

The other female passenger was dickering with the man from the livery for transportation to the hotel. Benton suggested, "Perhaps I should see if I can be of help to her."

"That won't be necessary, dear," his wife said frostily. "She appears to be quite capable of taking care of herself." They drove across town towards home.

The woman and her trunk were deposited by the livery dray on the front steps of the hotel. By the end of the short trip, the driver was so captivated by her he actually carried the trunk into the lobby.

The clerk behind the desk watched her cross the lobby, enthralled. Two men seated in a corner stopped talking to observe her arrival. She walked open and free, like a woman who controlled her own destiny and was happy about it.

She smiled at the clerk and asked, "Do you have a Frank Weston staying here? I am his aunt."

The clerk had to lick his suddenly dry lips twice before he was able to respond, "He left here several days ago."

She turned the register and picked up the pen. "When exactly did he leave?"

"Early in the morning, two days ago."

She was patient with him. "And where exactly did he go?"

"South is all I know. I wasn't around when he left. Mr. Karren might know. Do you want me to ask him?"

"Will this Mr. Karren be available later?"

"Yes. He's the owner of the hotel," he mumbled in explanation as she bent to pick up her small bag, distracting him.

"Then I will talk to him myself, later. I have had a long trip. Would you please send up a tub and hot water. I would like a bath."

"Of course. I'll see to it myself." He attempted to smooth his ragged moustache with his little finger. "If there is anything else I can do for you, feel free to ask."

Benton Stiles returned to the bank after lunch to find the woman from the train waiting for him, obviously enjoying the hostile regard of his secretary. She was dressed more formally than when he had seen her at the depot, but no clothing could disguise her vitality.

When they were seated in his office, she got right down to the point. "I have come about my brother's estate, Mr. Stiles. I know he made me executrix of his will and I want to make certain his property is transferred to Frank as quickly as possible."

"I am afraid there is very little left to transfer," he said nervously, watching her eyes widen in surprise. He explained in detail just what he had told Frank.

She sat in silence for a time while she thought over what he had told her. Reaching a decision she asked, "As I am legally responsible for the estate, would you mind if I looked at those loan papers?"

"Do you doubt what I say?" He was offended.

She smiled, disarmingly. "Of course not, Mr. Stiles. But I feel I have a duty to my nephew. I think I should see the papers in case there is any question later about the estate."

"Will you understand them?" he asked doubtfully.

"I have been a businesswoman for seventeen years, Mr. Stiles. I do know something about legal papers." She sat and waited, her soft brown eyes fixed on his face.

Stiles fidgeted for a few moments and then gave in. "I suppose there is no reason why you shouldn't." He was gone for several minutes. When he returned he carried a small file box. "I believe you will find everything pertaining to your brother's dealings with us in here."

She examined the contents of the box carefully, making notes on a sheet of paper she borrowed from the banker. He sat across the desk and tried to identify the items she was noting.

With a satisfied smile she replaced the papers in the file and sat back in her chair. "I realize I have already been a great deal of trouble to you, Mr. Stiles, but I do have to ask one more favor of you."

He basked in the warmth of her personality. "Of course. Whatever I can do."

"Would you give me time to arrange for the sale of the items on Franklin's farm not secured under the loan. I would like to obtain the best possible return for Frank, and one can never do that if one is in a hurry."

"That will be no trouble at all. It will be several months before we will be ready to sell that property, anyway. You take as much time as you need."

She stood and extended her hand. "You have been very kind. I hope I will be able to repay you somehow for all you have done for Franklin and his family."

He escorted her to the gate in the railing. "Please call on me for any assistance you may need while you are in Singleshoe. You will find me always available to you." He watched her walk away across the lobby with frank admiration.

Sheriff Carr was in his shirtsleeves cleaning a rifle when she entered his office. He examined her appreciatively as she introduced herself and then hurriedly donned his white doeskin jacket. "What can I do for you, Miss Stone?"

"It is about my brother. I have some questions I would like to ask you."

He was a bit wary. She was an entirely different matter from dealing with the boy. Her manner clearly showed that this woman knew what she was doing. "Have you talked to young Frank?" he asked cautiously.

"I haven't seen Frank in years, Sheriff, but I'm sure he acted a bit foolish while he was here. He always has been a bit of a snob. You have to keep in mind he has never been west and doesn't understand how things are done out here."

Carr relaxed. She had heard about his run-in with Frank and understood. This was a woman he could talk to man to man. "I heard he left town. That came as a surprise to me. He seemed to want to be here to make sure I did my job."

She smiled, disarmingly at him. "Perhaps he realized what a fool he was making of himself and decided it would be best if he stayed out of your way for a while. No one seems to know just where he has gone, though. Have you any idea?"

"All I know is he left on a freight wagon heading south. I wasn't interested in looking into it any further than that. The wagon stops at a number of small country stores on a circuit south of here. Perhaps he just went along for the ride."

Her brown eyes held his as he talked. He was finding her an exceptionally easy woman with which

66

to converse. "I want you to know he didn't have to leave town on my account. I admit I did get a bit angry with him, but I got over it."

"Of course you did, Sheriff. But that is not what I've come about. I want to check a couple of facts, and you seem to be the person who would know. My brother's will named me as executrix and I came here to settle his affairs." She relaxed in the chair, her expression open and aboveboard. "I understnd he was in the habit of loaning money to other farmers from time to time."

Carr studied her for a moment searching for the reason behind the question, but could not believe her guileless expression was hiding anything. "I heard he had. Did Benton tell you about it?"

"Yes, but not who they were. I would like to find that out so I can attempt to recover as much of the money as possible. It is my duty to my nephew."

He relaxed completely. She wasn't here to make trouble for him. "Of course I don't know who they all were. I just know about the ones who left town before he was killed." He wrote a list of names on the back of an old wanted poster and handed it across to her.

"You say none of these are still around?" she asked as she studied the list.

"All of them packed up and left soon after they talked your brother out of money. I don't like to speak ill of the dead, but your brother was an easy touch. He trusted everyone."

She looked up from the list, her expression suddenly cold. "Not quite everyone, Sheriff. My brother

67

and I were very close. Something around here was bothering him, so he forwarded a copy of any legal transactions he made to me for safekeeping. Everything. He didn't mention any of these men or the loan at the bank."

Standing, she slowly folded the list and placed it carefully in her bag. "My brother was a rich man, Sheriff. If he needed money all he had to do was notify his eastern bankers. He would never mortgage what was to be his and Agnes' final home."

Looking him directly in the eye, she continued, "There was something going on around here which he stumbled onto and it got him killed. I am not quite the innocent he was. It will be much more difficult to put me out of the way."

Walking quickly to the door she turned and said, "My death so soon after his would look very strange, wouldn't it, Sheriff?" Her eyes flashed as her control of the emotion behind them slipped for an instant. "I have a letter to mail to Denver. Would you be kind enough to direct me to the post office?"

He found his mouth was hanging open and had to consciously shut it before he could reply, "Left down the street to the depot."

The door shut firmly behind her and Sheriff Carr sat and stared unseeingly at it for a long time, deep in troubled thought. Finally, unable to convince himself she was no danger, he hurried across the street towards the bank to talk to Stiles. He was even more shaken to find her standing in front of the land office, watching him, a knowing smile on her lips.

CHAPTER SEVEN

Katherine was reaching for the handle of her hotel room door when she heard the sounds from inside. A muffled thud, as if someone had dropped a heavy object and a low curse.

She stood to one side and groped in her bag for the small derringer. Breaking it open, she checked the two cartridges. Then, slowly, careful not to make a sound, she turned the handle to free the latch and leave the door loose in her hand. The voice was clearer now. Whoever was talking was across the room near the window.

Thrusting the door open, she stepped inside, gun up and ready to fire.

The man stood in the dim light from the window examining the papers she had hidden under clothing in her trunk. When the door slammed back against the wall, he looked up, startled.

"You stay right where you are!" Katherine ordered.

A hand grabbed her wrist from behind, jerked the gun from her hand and flung her against the wall, the impact momentarily knocking the breath from her.

The second man advanced on her, hands balled into fists, a look on his face which didn't bode well for her.

"Be careful you don't hurt her, Jeff. Remember the orders." The man beside the window went back to reading the papers.

Katherine swung her heavy bag at the man's face when he came into range. He blocked it easily with his left forearm and dropped her with a short, vicious right. She was unconscious before she hit the floor.

She dreamt she was drowning and hands were clutching at her unable to help. Struggling for consciousness, she realized the water was in a cloth draped across her forehead and that someone was holding her hand and patting it cautiously.

"Miss Stone. Are you all right? Please speak to me." The voice was female and pleasant, though at the moment it was working its way towards hysterics.

Katherine opened her eyes to find the pretty dark-haired girl from the train leaning over her with a look of deep concern on her face. "Who are you?" she managed to ask before the pain in her jaw overwhelmed her.

"Emily Johnstone. What happened?"

Katherine struggled to sit up and Emily helped her into as comfortable a position as possible against the wall. She gingerly probed her jaw, testing to see if it was still in one piece. "That animal really slugged me. What time is it?"

The girl consulted a small watch pinned to the bodice of her dress. "Just after eight. Do you feel better now?"

"I've been out for more than an hour! The papers!" She struggled to get up from the floor. "Help me. I have to see if they found everything."

Emily reluctantly assisted her to her feet where she had to rest for a moment against the wall as a wave of dizziness swept through her. Then her excellent physical condition won out, her sense of balance returned and her eyesight cleared.

The debris of the men's search was scattered across the room, her traveling trunk turned upside down, clothing everywhere. She crossed to the open door and carefully closed it. "I had to talk tough to that Sheriff about what I was going to do. You would think by my age I would know when to keep my big mouth shut."

The carpetbag yielded a silver traveling flask. "I'm going to have a shot of whiskey. If your upbringing will be shocked, don't watch." She lowered the level in the bottle a healthy amount. With a contented sigh she recapped it and returned what remained to the bag. "Pardon my bad manners in not offering you any, but I have a feeling your mother has told you of the evils of drink. I don't want to put a temptation in your way."

She laughed at the confused look on Emily's face. "Don't mind me, honey. I'm just feeling a bit old and foolish." They straightened the room and repacked the trunk, finding, as she feared, the papers were all gone.

Katherine made Emily sit in the room's one chair while she perched on the bed. "Now, you tell me why you are here. I'm sure you don't normally spend your evenings prowling hotel hallways."

Emily giggled softly. "I just learned this afternoon that you were in town. I wanted to meet you and get to know you."

"I arrived on the same train you did. I would think that banker would have told you about me earlier. We had a talk the first afternoon I was in town. You are staying with him, aren't you?"

"Yes, I'm staying with the Stiles. This is part of what bothers me. They didn't say anything at all to me about you. May, their daughter, heard them talking about you and thought I would like to know." She looked a little bewildered. "I really don't understand why they didn't tell me."

"I think I have a pretty good idea. They don't want the two of us to get together." She studied Emily thoughtfully for a moment. "I am going to tell you something which will be hard for you to accept. You will have to take my word for it because the two men who knocked me out were here to steal what proof I had."

"Mama always said you were not a liar, no matter what else you were."

Katherine laughed. "I bet she said a good deal more than that about me." She sobered suddenly and began, "My brother, Frank's father was on to some kind of crooked scheme that was going on around here. Someone was using fear to chase families off the better pieces of land. It looked like whoever was doing it was putting together an extensive piece of property."

"Did he know who it was?" Emily's curiosity made her lean forward with excitement.

"He suspected Benton Stiles was behind it."

"The banker? That couldn't be. His wife went to school with my mother!"

"I'm afraid attending Laurel Heights is not exactly an iron-clad reference. Franklin had gathered proof and begun to fear he would be next. He sent it all on to me with instructions as to what to do if anything happened to him."

Emily breathed, "And then they killed him."

"Yes." Katherine shook her head in disgust. "I decided I knew better than anyone what to do and came down here all by myself to see justice done. I talked big to the Sheriff and let him see me going into the land office. You have seen what resulted."

"They got all the proof?"

Katherine nodded glumly.

"But why didn't you put it in a safe place, like the bank, or..." She giggled self-consciously. "I guess you couldn't very well put evidence against Mr. Stiles in his own bank for safekeeping, could you? What are we going to do now?"

Pleased by the "we" Katherine said, "You are going back to the Stiles and behave as if you knew nothing about any of this."

"I can't do that. How could I face them when I know they killed Frank's family?"

"Just continue to act as you have been. You are a smart, pretty girl. Smart, pretty girls have advantages. Use them. Don't try to put anything over on Matilda Stiles, though. If she is involved in this she will see right through you."

"Do you think she is?"

"I really don't know, but I have a feeling she isn't. She is the type that lives to see her daughter do better than she did. Something like this would ruin her chances forever."

Emily nodded. "She wants my mother to look after May when she goes back to Laurel Heights to school year after next. She wouldn't chance anything happening to that arrangement. Maybe I can find some proof if I search Mr. Stiles' study. He seems to keep a lot of private papers there."

"You be careful. It will be better if they don't know you suspect them. One of them might say something useful in your hearing. Besides, it would be dangerous for you if they found out."

"I'll be careful," Emily promised. "What are you going to do?"

Katherine smiled and changed the subject. "Do you know about Frank?"

All other thoughts instantly fled Emily's head. "Where is he? Is he all right? I've been so worried and no one seems to know anything about him."

"The man who owns this hotel, Will Karren, says he told Frank about a man who might help him look into the killings. A gunfighter named Luther North who lives a couple of day's ride south of here. Will made arrangements for Frank to ride a freight wagon down to see him."

"Is he all right?"

"From what I have been able to learn, he is fine. Some of the Sheriff's deputies beat him up to make him leave town, but Will says there was no real damage."

"Thank goodness. I have been so worried, and all Mr. Stiles could or would tell me was Frank had gone south."

"I hope that is all he knows," Katherine said seriously. "And that is all he must find out."

"He won't learn anything from me. You can be sure of that."

"I can tell you have heard something positive just by the way you are acting. Now that you know he is safe you have gone all cheerful and that worried look you wore when you came in here is gone. You are going to have to be careful not to seem too happy. Remember you don't know anything so you should be worried. Don't go around singing and laughing for heaven's sake."

Emily put on a mock worried expression which

dissolved quickly into giggles. "I'll practice looking serious on my way home. I won't give you away."

"I'm sure you won't, Emily. If you should let it slip, though, don't tell them you got it from me. They mustn't even know we have talked. Now you better get on back before they start to worry about you." She led Emily to the back stairs. "It will be best if you aren't seen leaving the hotel. Benton Stiles is not stupid. He can put two and two together as well as any man."

Emily kissed her fondly on the cheek. "I like you, Aunt Katherine. Frank is lucky to have you in his family. How do I get in touch with you if I find out something?"

"Don't try. I'll find a way to contact you. It will be safer for both of us that way."

As Emily started down the steps Katherine put out a hand to restrain her. "You might hear some bad things about me in the next few days. Please remember. I will do anything to find the men who killed my brother and his family."

CHAPTER EIGHT

Luther North was contentedly soaking the recently healed scars of several bullet wounds in the shallows near one edge of his ranch pond when the boy's body hurtled through the air to land in the center of the expanse of still water.

The satisfied laugh which followed him across the water·told Luther that Jester had provided the propelling force. The turbulence the boy stirred up with his panicked struggles disturbed the surface badly enough so that Luther had to reach out a hand to steady the small float on which rode the bottle of whiskey, the glass and the waterproof packet of cigars which made his daily dip in the pond more enjoyable.

From above him the same satisfied voice called, "You wanted to see Luther, boy. Look around. He's in there somewhere." The laughter rumbled across the water again.

Luther swam slowly out of the shade into the sunlit center of the pond and looked up at the stocky old man who stood, hands on hips, on the bank.

"What the hell is going on, Jester?"

The old man's pale eyes shifted their focus from the boy's struggles to Luther. "This young gentleman wanted to see you, Luther. Matter of fact, he insisted on it. Said he don't deal with servants." The young gentleman in question had disappeared beneath the surface.

"Why did you bring him down here? Couldn't you just chase him off like you're supposed to?" Luther knew exactly why Jester had brought the boy here. He wasn't a man that would take kindly to being called a servant.

The boy reappeared, flailing around and trying desperately to attract Luther's attention.

He ignored him "What are you going to do about him?" he demanded of Jester.

The old man shrugged indifferently as the boy sank beneath the surface for the second time. "Not a damn thing, Luther. You're out there. If you think someone should do something, you do it."

As Luther swore with considerable feeling at him

he suddenly realized there was no other sound from the pond. The surface was again calm and undisturbed where the boy had been. He swam over and peered down through the clear water.

About eight feet down the boy's body hung suspended, his reddish-brown hair floating in a cloud around his head. There was no apparent motion.

Luther kicked over and dove down to grab the body by the seat of the pants. He pulled the dead weight to the surface and towed it across to the bank where a suddenly subdued Jester helped drag him out.

"Is he dead?"

"If not, he's as close as he will ever get. Help me roll him over that log."

Several anxious minutes followed before the boy suddenly gagged violently and spewed up a thick stream of water. Luther stepped well clear while Jester pounded him heavily on the back to assist his breathing.

The boy endured the assault for a couple of minutes before he finally began to feebly rebel. He rolled off the log and sat miserably in the ruins of his expensive suit. After a time his breathing settled into a more normal pattern and the colar began to return to his pasty-white face.

"You all right?" Jester asked.

"No thanks to you. Why did you throw me in there? I can't swim." He was growing angry now the danger was past.

"You wanted to see Luther. That's where he was," Jester replied innocently, his relief over the boy's recovery tempered by a return of his irritation with his manner.

The boy finally noticed the naked man standing in the shade beneath a tree. Big, a good six foot tall, well muscled, the white scars of a number of knife and bullet wounds standing out against his well tanned body.

"Are you Luther North?" he demanded.

Luther remembered he was naked, reached down a towel from the tree and began to rub himself dry. "I am," he admitted reluctantly.

The boy struggled to his feet and stood swaying until he recovered his sense of balance. Then he advanced on Luther who was fastening up an old pair of denim pants. "I am Frank Weston. I want to hire you to do a job for me."

"What kind of job?" Luther asked warily.

"I need a man who is good with a gun. Will Karren in Singleshoe says you are the best there is."

Luther picked up a long stick and walked to the edge of the pond where he used it to pull the whiskey float over to the bank. "I only work for the government," he said, concentrating on the float.

Frank laughed knowingly, "I'm sure you will be willing to work for me when you learn how much I am willing to pay."

"I don't work for private individuals," Luther repeated.

"Oh, come now," Frank scoffed. "You mean to tell me a man in your line of work would turn me down just because I don't happen to be a government. I told you I am willing to pay you enough money to make it worth your while."

Luther picked up the half-empty whiskey bottle, stuck the glass between his elbow and side and bent for the packet of cigars with his remaining hand. The glass slipped free and fell to the ground at the edge of the pond. There was a trace of exasperation in his voice as he said, "It doesn't make the slightest bit of difference how much money you want to pay me. I don't work for private individuals. The answer is no and will remain no. Don't push it any further."

"Don't give me that," Frank said scornfully. "A hired gun is a hired gun. You make your living using it for people who can afford to pay your price."

Luther bent for the glass and Frank impatiently kicked it out from under his hand and into the pond.

"I will pay you more than your usual rate," the boy continued. "I know you have a price, so why don't we just skip all the bargaining you usually go through to protect your pride and I will agree to whatever amount you set."

He dusted his hands together distastefully as if he had just handled a particularly dirty job. "Now that that is settled let's go to a more comfortable place and I will tell you exactly what I want you to do."

Luther watched the glass slowly fill with water and sink out of sight. Then he handed the bottle and cigars to the obviously amused Jester and turned to grasp Frank's coat firmly by the soggy lapels. He jerked him well clear of the ground and pulled him close.

"I swim in that pond every day, you little ass. I like it nice and clean. When someone clutters it up with trash it irritates the hell out of me." The boy's eyes grew wide as he suddenly realized how angry Luther was.

"When I get irritated someone often gets hurt," Luther continued dangerously. "You're going to find that glass and bring it up to the house for me to see or I will show you just exactly how a hired gun behaves when he is mad."

He slowly turned the boy in his hands until he had him by the collar and the seat of the pants. Then he threw him back into the pond so he landed exactly where the glass had disappeared from sight.

"You make damn sure you come out of there with that glass!" he ordered harshly and turned to stalk off across the pasture towards the house.

Only then did the boy's shock wear off enough for panic to set in. He began to thrash around wildly and yell for help.

Jester had watched the scene with appreciation and now followed Luther across the pasture. "What if he drowns?" he asked.

"Then we'll bury him somewhere and you can go in after the glass." Luther's temper was still showing.

"Me? Why me?" Jester knew better than to push Luther in this mood, but he couldn't help himself.

"You brought that obnoxious little bastard down to the pond in the first place. If you had just run him off like you were supposed to, this wouldn't have happened."

The yelling from the pond stopped and in the sudden silence Jester considered what Luther had said. "Then I sure hope he brings it out," he said with feeling. Jester didn't much like large bodies of water. "Do you think he will?"

"If he has the sense God gave a grasshopper he will stand up and find out the water is only three feet deep where he is. If he doesn't, he deserves to drown."

"What do you want me to do with him when he comes up to the house?"

"Have Ma dry that ridiculous suit and ask him to supper. We might as well feed him before you make sure he leaves here by a route which will prevent him ever finding his way back."

CHAPTER NINE

Luther took his time changing to give his anger a chance to cool and walked through the rambling adobe house to the kitchen where he found Ma arranging young Weston's damp clothing on an improvised rack in front of her oven.

"Where's Jester?" he asked.

"Went out to take care of the team that boy drove in here. He didn't want to leave them standing out in the heat of the day while we ate." She pointed to the sink. "The boy brought in that glass and said to make sure you knew about it." She contemplated him severely. "What did you do to scare him so bad?"

"He kicked the glass in the pond. I threw him in after it."

"You did more than that. You half-scared him to death."

"I guess he did rile me some. I don't much like being told by some fresh kid that I'm only a hired gun available to anyone with the money to buy me."

"I see." Her stern expression softened. "You and Jester are too touchy about what people think. He's just some confused kid who doesn't know any better. They don't have people like you back where he comes from."

She returned to her preparations for supper. After a time she spoke again, "Why don't you go out on the porch and listen to his story. It won't hurt you none and it could do him some good. There is a lot of pain built up in that boy. Maybe you can help him get rid of some of it."

Luther walked over and put an arm around her ample waist. "I don't suppose Will would have sent him down here if he didn't think it was important."

She slapped his hand away good-naturedly. "You get on out of my kitchen so I can get some work done. There were some nice lemons in the supplies this time. I'll make some lemonade and bring it out to you."

The boy was huddled in a chair in the far corner of the porch. When the door clicked shut behind Luther he looked up and nervously pulled the blanket in which he was wrapped closer. "I gave your glass to the woman in the kitchen."

"She showed it to me." Luther pulled a chair across to where he could lean back, his feet propped on the railing. "You feeling all right now?"

"What do you care? I could have drowned in that pond when you walked away and left me."

Shaking his head with amusement Luther said, "Why don't you cut out all this angry talk, Frank. You are not back where your family is important enough for you to get away with it. Out here it just rubs people the wrong way."

The boy slowly began to relax. "I suppose I do talk a little strong," he admitted seriously. "But I never tried to hire a gunfighter before."

Luther laughed, "We'll get along much better if you quit calling me a gunfighter. I don't spend my days wandering the countryside putting on fast-draw exhibitions and shooting people."

Frank had the grace to blush. "I guess that is how I've been thinking of you. I'm sorry. I'll apologize to your man, also."

"That is another thing, Frank. You seem to look on Jester as a servant or something. I live here with him and Ma as equals. If you don't want to go back in the pond, I would keep that in mind."

Luther settled a bit lower in the chair. "Why don't you tell me why you came all the way out here to hire me."

Frank sat up in excitement, losing his grip on the blanket which fell open to reveal his bruised chest. "Then you'll help me?"

"Hold on now. I didn't say anything of the kind. Ma thinks it would be good for you to get whatever it is that is bothering you out in the open. There might even be some way I could help if I knew what the problem was."

"I don't suppose it would do any harm to tell you," he said thoughtfully. "Do you have a lot of friends in Singleshoe?"

"Other than Mary Kate and her girls or Will Karren at the hotel I don't know anyone there except to speak to. Why?"

"Mr. Karren is the one sent me down to talk to you. We had a long talk after I got there," he gestured at the bruises, "And found we had the same suspicions. And of the same people."

"That is a mark in your favor. Will is not a man to jump to conclusions."

Jester was walking across the yard from the barn and Ma came out of the kitchen with a pitcher of lemonade. Luther suggested, "Why don't you tell all of us at once. I would just tell them later, anyway, and the three of us might be of more help than me alone."

Frank waited until the two were settled before he began, "First, I want to tell you this country is completely strange to me. There is a lot I don't understand, so if I have put a foot wrong anywhere, I apologize."

Jester nodded and Ma smiled warmly. "Don't you worry, Frank. You are among friends here."

Frank seemed comforted by her manner. He smiled shyly at her and continued, "My father,

Franklin Weston, bought a farm north of Single-shoe early last year. You may of heard of him?" He looked around the circle and seemed surprised when none of them had.

"Our family has been in the banking business in the east for years and done very well. My father took over from his father and prospered, but he was never really happy. What he wanted most was to be a farmer and work outside. Not in our part of the country where the farms are small, but out here where there was lots of room. He studied all the information he could find and experimented at our country place until he came to believe he could farm profitably on the plains. Then he and my mother decided to move west. I know she approved, though I never really understood why. Frankly, I had no interest in ever coming west. There would be a place for me in the family business when I graduated, so, other than missing my family, I agreed they should try it.

"My father had several friends in this part of the country, and they kept their eyes open for the kind of property he needed. By Christmas two years ago he had learned of three places which interested him. He made a trip out here that winter and found the one north of Singleshoe just what he wanted. That March he and my mother, my sisters Mary and Ruth and my youngest brother James moved out here.

"They hired a man to help and he and my father got in the first year's crop. It did better than even my father had hoped. He wrote in his letters how many of the things he had experimented with back east had worked. He was looking forward to sharing his ideas with his neighbors.

"That first year he spent a large sum on the farm, making it the home in which he and mother planned to live out their lives."

"And that brought on trouble with the neighbors," Jester guessed.

Frank shook his head, "No. If you had known my parents you would never think that. They got on well with everyone. The only stuffed shirt in the family is me."

Luther sat up a little straighter. Frank had said if they "had known" his parents.

"My father's letters began to mention trouble," Frank continued, "Though not for him. Whole families were disappearing and no one would ever hear of them again. On each farm the barn would be burned. The Sheriff hired a number of deputies, but never seemed to be able to find out what was happening."

"Henry Carr couldn't find himself if he was the only man in a room," Jester growled. "I wouldn't trust him to hold my horse."

"Now Jester," Ma said quietly. From the look on her face Luther knew she had caught the "had known" also. "You let Frank tell his story. He isn't interested in what you think of the Sheriff."

Frank was staring at Jester. "But I am. I happen to agree, though I think it goes deeper than his just being incompetent."

"What about the rest of your family?" Luther

asked. "Do they think something is wrong, also?"

"My sisters and brother thought they had found the promised land. My mother was one of those mothers who only wrote happy, positive letters. She might have hinted at problems, but I was courting a girl at the time and would have missed anything which wasn't very plain."

He looked down across the pasture to the trees around the pond. Ma asked softly, "What happened to the girl?"

"Emily? We became engaged three weeks ago. The telegram arrived while we were having the celebration at her parent's home."

He had to clear his throat a couple of times before he could continue. "A gang of men rode onto the farm three weeks ago and killed my family and the hired man." He shook his head suddenly and the moisture in his eyes glinted in the afternoon sunlight. "No. That is not quite accurate. Mary killed Ruth and then herself to save them from those men after my parents were dead. The murderers even shot the old dog James had had since he was born."

"What did Sheriff Carr do?" Jester's voice was strained.

"As near as I can find out, he didn't do much of anything. He told me the killers didn't leave any trace of who they were or where they went. I don't think he really had any desire to catch them. His deputies seem to spend all their time in town drinking and gambling. They are the ones gave me this beating when I confronted them."

He was talking a bit easier now. "When I arrived

in Singleshoe I went to the bank to see Mr. Stiles about the estate. He told me there was very little left. He had a loan agreement which he said my father had signed when he borrowed money for the improvements on the farm. If I wasn't going to continue to pay on it, the bank would foreclose to get its money back. Also, there was very little money left in the personal account. Mr Stiles said my father used to loan money to men who couldn't qualify for loans at the bank. He said my father was too trusting a man and people took advantage of him."

"You don't think he is telling the truth about the land or the money, do you?" Luther asked quietly.

"I told you earlier my father was a rich man. He wrote me several times he was paying for everything as he went along. He realized there were a lot of things which could happen to a man in this country and he wanted to make sure my mother would have no trouble over the farm if something did happen to him. Then there are the men to whom my father is supposed to have loaned money."

"They won't admit to it?"

"They all seem to be the same men who left the country with no trace."

"Damn convenient," Jester muttered.

They sat for several minutes in silence while each thought over the story. Frank asked, finally, "Will you come back to Singleshoe and help me find out who is really responsible for what happened to my family, Mr. North?"

Luther started to answer, but Ma forestalled him, "It's time for supper, Frank. We will all feel better after a good meal."

She turned to Luther. "It's been some time since you paid a visit to your lady friends at that place in Singleshoe. If you got a good start right after supper, the two of you could spend the night with the Polks and be in town tomorrow afternoon."

Luther raised an eyebrow in surprise.

"You wouldn't be hiring out to Frank," she explained calmly. "He can just ride back with you. If anything should happen to him, you would be right there. That is, when you aren't in that woman's place."

Luther grinned suddenly. "I think I better get my things together, Frank. This will probably be the only time I will ever get to visit Mary Kate with Ma's blessing."

CHAPTER TEN

The light spring wagon steadily across the deserted prairie, each mile much like the last. The sparse covering of prairie grass tinted the grey-brown land with a pale green, accented with splotches of darker green by the bolder soapweed and hardier prairie fauna. Since leaving Polks early that morning Luther and Frank had made good time. Amos Polk had replaced Frank's ruined suit with heavy corduroy pants and a sturdy wool work shirt. The new on them could be heard every time

Frank shifted position, but he was obviously pleased with the total change from the clothing he was used to.

Luther drove, following the faint double trace which connected Polks with the Singleshoe stage road. Frank either dozed or stared at the rolling plains. They had seen no other traveler since they left Polks and they seemed to be all alone in the world.

Just after eleven they stopped to eat the lunch put up by Mrs. Polk and then moved on, wanting to reach Singleshoe as early in the afternoon as possible. Frank spotted the first living things he had seen that day, hundreds of small creatures perched on mounds around the mouths of the burrows which infested a flat field the road was skirting. The animals seemed unafraid, though relaxed their vigilance while the wagon was near.

"Prarie dogs," Luther explained laconically.

They were the first words he had spoken in hours and Frank determined to take advantage of the opening. "Why do you live so far from anywhere?" he asked.

Luther remained silent for such a long time Frank decided he was going to ignore the question. He said, finally, "I like my privacy. Besides, I have made a few enemies over the years. They would have a tough time getting to me out there."

"I don't think I understand."

"You may not have realized it, but the Polk's store is on the highest ground for miles around. No one can approach my valley without being observed. My mail also comes to their store, and they handle our supplies for us. Just enough people frequent the store to provide a reason for its existance and I pay them well on top of that to stay alert. No one can get into my valley during the day without my having plenty of warning."

"What happens after dark?"

"You don't see the dogs. We turn them loose when it gets dark. They know Jester, Ma and me. Anyone else would have a real problem if they came on them running free. Nobody is going to get in past them undetected."

"How did you find a place like that?" Frank's curiosity had been growing for hours.

"Jester knew about it from back in the fifties when he lived with the Cheyenne and roamed this whole country. I helped him out of a tough spot during a fight in a saloon in Black Hawk after the war and he stayed with me. He's damn good in a fight and loyal, even if he is a bit hard to live with."

"Is Ma his wife?"

Luther laughed. "Frankly, I don't know. The year after we built the house, Jester disappeared for a couple of months. When he came back she was with him. I never felt it was my place to inquire about their relationship. I'm just happy to have her around. It makes the place a good deal more civilized."

"It sounds like you like her."

"She is the reason I'm going back with you, that and the fact that I've been cooped up on the ranch too long and need to get into town and howl."

Frank sat very stiffly, "I thought you were going because you believed my story."

"I listened to it. I didn't believe or disbelieve. I'll decide when I have more facts."

"You are a cold man, Mr. North," Frank stated bitterly.

Luther looked at him for a moment. "Just careful, Frank. There are any number of people who would be delighted to see me dead and would be willing to go to almost any lengths to accomplish it. For all I know you could be the bait in a trap."

Frank rode in silence for several minutes. "Do you really think I am?" he asked seriously.

"No," Luther laughed. "But I'll be careful anyway."

"What would happen if I were?"

"You would be dead before you could enjoy whatever you were paid."

A shiver ran down his spine at the tone of Luther's voice, and Frank turned to look at him. "Why don't you think I am?"

"For one thing, Will Karren sent you down. He is a good man and I trust him. For another, if they wanted to lure me into a trap there is much better bait than you."

They rode for several miles in silence.

The two mounted men were waiting for them when they emerged from the mouth of the draw the road had followed between two converging hills. Luther was concerned about one of the horses which seemed to be laboring a bit in the rough spots and was not as alert as he should have been.

One was planted firmly in the center of the road pointing a shotgun directly at Luther. The second man rode slowly along the side of the wagon until he could look directly down at Frank.

"If it isn't young Mr. Weston. I see our first warning wasn't strong enough, boy. You didn't go back east like you were told." He smiled a cold, unpleasant smile. "I'm going to make you wish you had." He spat on the front wheel. "And this time there won't be any nosey hotelkeeper to interfere where he isn't wanted."

He shifted his attention to Luther. "Your a friend of Weston here?"

Luther tried to appear scared, "I just picked him up at Polks. Amos said he rode down on a freight wagon and he wanted him back in town. I was just doing him a favor." He looked from one man to the other. "What's this all about, anyway?"

The man studied him for a long moment. "Something about you bothers me, mister. We ever met before?"

He leaned forward to get a closer look at Luther. Frank reached up, grabbed him by the shirt and jerked hard.

Luther yelled violently at the team and slapped them viciously with the loose ends of the reins. They sprang forward, catching the man in the middle of the road unprepared, knocking both he and his horse to one side. Frank couldn't hold onto the gunmen when the wagon lurched ahead, so he had to let him drop over the side.

They came up out of the small valley at a dead

run, the team lunging madly at the harness. Luther handed the reins to Frank and ordered, "Keep them moving. I want to have a short visit with those two."

As the wagon passed around a sharp bend it slewed wildly in the loose sand of the road, the horses had to scramble for footing, slowing the speed. Luther jumped from the seat, landing on his shoulder and rolling into cover. Lying on his back in the shelter of the hill he checked the cartridges in his revolver.

A moment later the rattle of the wagon and the metalic jingle of the harness was replaced by the erratic drum beat of the two horsemen as they pursued. He climbed the slope of the hill until he was ten feet above the level of the road.

When the men passed below he shot the lead horse in the head, collapsing the animal in a floundering heap. The second rider, the one who had come down the wagon to threaten Frank, had to work frantically with his legs and hands to keep his horse upright. Successful, he turned back towards Luther, gun in hand.

He had waited to see the results of his first shot, wanting the man to know who was about to kill him. The man's gun came up and Luther shot him twice in the chest.

The other man was crawling slowly away from his horse in the direction of the shotgun, dragging a broken leg. Luther slid down the side of the hill in his direction.

He would have caught him before he could get to the gun, but his foot caught in the exposed roots of a clump of grass. The man grabbed for the gun desperately and rolled over onto his back.

Luther jerked his boot free and launched himself feet first towards the gun. Flying through the air he heard the marked clicks as the man cocked the hammers. The exposed soft places of his body tingled in anticipation as they awaited the impact of the buckshot.

His left boot struck the barrel of the gun just as the man pulled the triggers, deflecting the blast to one side where it cut a swath through the sharp leaves of a soapweed plant.

His right boot connected with the side of the man's jaw, breaking it in two places and knocking him unconscious.

Luther tended to the wounded man and wrapped the dead one in his bedroll tarp. He was using the remaining animal to drag the dead horse from the road when Frank returned with the wagon.

The college boy could only sit and stare slack-jawed at the scene of sudden carnage.

Luther tossed him a shiny star. "Recognize that?"

"A deputy's badge?"

He nodded. "Were these two part of the gang who beat you up?"

"The one who talked to us was. I don't remember the other one."

"That means they have more than the six men you saw before. Keep that badge. I don't want Henry Carr to suspect I know they are his deputies. Besides, I know the dead one."

"There are two men in my wagon, one dead and the other with a broken jaw. I want the injured one charged with robbery and attempted murder. I don't much care what you do with the dead one, just get him out of my wagon."

Sheriff Carr hurried outside to examine the two men. Luther had dropped Frank off at the rear door of the hotel before bringing the wagon around to the Sheriff's office. He had no intention of telling Henry anything more than was absolutely necessary.

The Sheriff lifted a corner of the tarp. "That's Jeff Coats. What did he do?"

"He and his friend stopped me about five miles south of town and said they were going to kill me. They were damned inept about it, though. Maybe they thought I was easy pickings. Coats was never much on smart." He watched Carr lift the man with the broken jaw out of the wagon. "What is this country coming to when a man can't even ride up here for a little amusement without being held up. You should chase some of this riff-raff away, Henry."

The Sheriff retreated under the verbal assault. "I don't understand it, Luther. Why would they stop you? They've always been good boys as far as I know."

"That's crap, Henry, and you know it. Coats is wanted in half the states between the Missouri and the Pacific. I bet you've got a wanted poster on him in your office right this minute. If you've been letting him hang around town, you've been neglecting your

duty. I'm surprised he hasn't robbed or killed someone before this."

Henry sputtered, "You can't talk to me like that,
Luther. I'm the Sheriff of this county. That office is
due some respect."

"I'll talk to you any way I damn please, Henry.
I'm the one he held up. How would you like it if I
wired Denver and complained about the way you do
your job?"

The Sheriff backed off, "Now, Luther. You don't
want to get carried away. We've known each other a
long time," he continued soothingly. "Too long to
let a thing like this come between us."

"I suppose so," Luther agreed reluctantly. "I
didn't come up to Singleshoe to get in a fight. You
can use my wagon to transport this garbage to Clarence's, then leave it at the livery with Cam. I'm going
to be around for a couple of days before I go home,
so if you want me, I'll be at the hotel."
He turned and stalked off up the street, the Sheriff
staring after him. If those two punks had gotten
Luther North involved! After a careful search of the
men's pockets he heaved a sigh of relief. At least they
had sense enough not to carry their badges. That
would really have set Luther off.

"What happened?"

Henry turned at the sound of Benton Stiles' voice.
"I sent a couple of men down to take care of Frank
Weston. They must have taken on Luther North by
mistake."

"Does he suspect they work for us?"

"I don't think so or he would have said something

to me. He isn't a man to wait. He also isn't a man to mix much in private affairs."

"See that he isn't given any further provocation," Stiles ordered. "Keep your men away from him." He started to turn away and stopped. "Except for Banks."

"Banks?"

"I want to know everything North does while he is in town. Banks can keep track of him without his knowing it. He mustn't suspect a thing."

CHAPTER ELEVEN

"Get your party clothes on, Frank. We're going to have some fun tonight." Luther chuckled, "You must have another pretty suit like the one you wore down to my place."

Luther and Frank were in Will Karren's private rooms behind the front desk of the hotel. The boy wasn't very enthusiastic, but Will urged him to go. "You can't stay cooped up around here forever. It will do you good to get out."

'I just got engaged three weeks ago and you want

me to go to a place like that!" Frank was appalled.

"Don't be so straight-laced," Will said with a grin. "You don't have to do anything and it will be more interesting than hanging around here watching me count the laundry."

"You can just sit back in Mary Kate's private parlor and visit, Frank. No one will know you are there and I'll have a better time knowing you are safe. After this afternoon's little fracas I have to admit I worry some. You don't seem to have made many friends here in Singleshoe."

"Come on, Luther. They wouldn't try anything here in town. Not with you around."

"Don't be too sure, boy. Now get ready. I don't intend to take no for an answer."

"I guess it couldn't hurt anything," Frank conceded. "I suppose I could go." He went back to his room to change.

"Mary Kate has a friend visiting her from St. Louis," Will told Luther. "You tell her you want to meet Katherine. That I suggested it. This is a woman you will like, Luther. You miss her and you'll regret it."

Luther slapped him on the shoulder in thanks. "Will, I can almost forgive you for sicking the boy on me." He adjusted his hat to just the right angle and called impatiently, "Come on, Frank. It's getting late." He was whistling softly as he left.

Mary Kate's black maid answered Luther's knock on the house's private entrance. "Mr. Luther! You come on in here, and welcome." She caught sight of the boy behind him. "Who's your friend?"

"This is Frank, Dot. How've you been?" He patted her ample rear fondly. "You're still the most exciting woman in the place. When are you going to take up the trade?"

"You go on now!" she simpered. "I'll just put you here in the parlor and go fetch Miss Kate. Would you gentlemen like some refreshment while you wait?"

"You know what I want, Dot. Bring some cold tea for my young friend here. I promised I would keep him out of trouble."

"Then he's sure with the wrong man," she suggested with a giggle.

They had to wait several minutes before a tiny woman in her late thirties swept into the room, the cloud of silk which floated around her just barely concealing the important parts of her exquisite body. Her slightly overdone makeup carefully disguised the hard lines of her face from all but the closest examination.

Luther enfolded her in a crushing embrace which she responded to a bit more than her profession required. It was several moments before she noticed Frank standing self-consciously across the room. She stepped away from Luther and the natural pleasure of her greeting for him was replaced by a mask of professional enthusiasm.

"Mary Kate," Luther introduced. "This is Frank Weston. I'm kind of looking out for him."

The name brought a gleam to her eyes. "Welcome to my house, Frank. I'm sure we have someone here who will interest you." There was an amused shading to her voice.

Frank awkwardly accepted the small hand she extended. "Actually, ma'am, I'm not here to see a girl." He stammered, dropped his hat and had to bend to pick it up which made him even more embarrassed.

Luther put an arm around her tiny waist. "Frank is just out from the east. He has had some troubles, and I want to keep him where he is safe while I have a little fun. He just got engaged three weeks ago and is feeling very loyal to his girl."

She smiled mischieviously, "We can put him in my private parlor. No one goes in there unless I say they can." She grasped Luther's arm with both hands, hugging it to her warm body. "What about you, Luther? Do you want a girl or did you come here to just sit in my parlor too."

Luther laughed. "You know damn well what I came here for, Mary Kate. Will Karren said I should ask about your new girl, Katherine. He says she is something special."

Mary Kate looked up at him speculatively. "She is, Luther, she is. Come this way." Her bright invitation included them both.

She led them through a curtained archway and paused to knock lightly on a door. Then she pushed it open and said, "Katherine, this is Luther North. Will Karren recommended him." She stepped to one side to allow Luther to enter.

The woman had been reading in a chair in the far corner. When Mary Kate knocked she had stepped into the shadows out of the circle of light cast by the room's single burning lamp. As she stepped back into view Luther couldn't suppress a sudden intake of breath. She was spectacular. Tall, plainly dressed in a simple grey frock which fit perfectly from neck to hips and then hung straight to the floor. A cloud of reddish-brown hair flowed down across her shoulders, framing a face without makeup. She was lightly tanned, a few freckles adding interest to the alert brown eyes, pert nose and full lips.

"Luther, this is Katherine Stone," Mary Kate said.

He started across the room towards her in a bit of a daze. What a woman like this was doing in Mary Kate's place he didn't know, but he intended to take full advantage of her presence. Frank's first words, however, brought him up short.

"Aunt Katherine!"

He stood frozen, a strange look crossing his face. He turned to glare at Mary Kate and was surprised by the motherly look she had acquired as she looked from the boy to his aunt.

"What are you doing in a place like this?" Frank demanded as he crossed the room.

Katherine smiled at him, "I've been waiting for you to return with Mr. North, Frank. Are you all right? Will told me you had been badly beaten." Her sudden concern broke the boy's resistance and his slow progress became a dash to the shelter of her arms.

Mary Kate sniffed back a tear and patted Luther tenderly on the arm. "You help her, Luther. She needs you."

"But, Mary Kate. I didn't come here for this kind of thing. What about the entertainment you promised?"

"Not tonight, Luther. You listen to what she has to say." He had seen that same look on Ma's face when she told him to come to town with the boy. His feelings of gratitude towards Will were undergoing rapid revision.

Turning on Frank and his aunt he asked in some confusion, "Just what is going on here?"

She advanced across the room to meet him, still holding Frank's hand. "Will and Mary Kate felt this was the safest place for me to wait until Frank returned with you. I am so pleased you have decided to help us."

Even Frank could sense the affect his spectacular aunt was having on Luther. For the first time he saw her as something other than the bright, fun woman who came to visit them and was able to do all the things which interested a child. He now saw her as Luther did and was a little in awe.

When Luther didn't reply he explained, "Mr. North hasn't decided whether to help us yet, Aunt Katherine. He wants to find out more about it first."

She didn't take her eyes from Luther's face. "Then why don't you sit over here on the couch beside me, Mr. North. Frank, you sit in the chair under the light." She took Luther's arm with a small, firm hand and guided him to the couch. Even after they were seated her hand remained lightly on his forearm. Luther could sense her across the few inches which separated them like a moth senses light. The spot where her fingers maintained their gentle contact seemed to glow.

Her voice was low, warm and vibrant as she continued, "We will tell him all we know, Frank. Then I am sure he will help us."

As he watched the two, Frank was also sure. All his life he had looked on his aunt as just his father's sister. This woman was totally in command of herself and focusing her entire personality on Luther. Even to a bystander the affect was overwhelming. He didn't think Luther had much of a chance.

Then, suddenly, the contact between the two was broken. Luther sat back and, after looking at Katherine for permission, lit a cigar. "Do you remember what I was telling you about bait in a trap, Frank?" He continued to concentrate on the woman, a slight smile on his lips. "I told you anyone who knew me could come up with better bait than you. Now you can see what I was talking about."

"You consider me bait in a trap, Mr. North?" she asked softly, both hands now lying quietly in her lap, though her eyes were still fixed on his.

"Aren't you?"

She laughed a low, throaty laugh, "Of course I am."

Frank sat forward abruptly, "Aunt Katherine!"

She looked over at him for a moment and then returned her attention to Luther. "But I am, Frank. We want Mr. North to help us. If he does it because of me or for what I am, it will still be what we want." She continued to regard Luther calmly. "He and I understand each other, Frank. If I am the bait he needs to help us, then that is the way it will be."

Luther laughed openly, head back, his expression one of appreciation. "I will be damned, Aunt Katherine. I'm not sure what I'm letting myself in for, but, to use Frank's words, you have got yourself a gunfighter."

The two sat and looked at one another for a long time, their interest in each other totally shutting out a now bewildered Frank.

"I'm not making any promises in return, Luther," she said softly, using his given name for the first time.

"I don't expect any." He reached across and took her hand. "Whatever happens between us will be outside of this."

The heavy emotion in the room suddenly lifted and he continued in a much calmer voice, "Now tell me what you know about this."

CHAPTER TWELVE

"Don't you ever speak to me again, Frank Weston! How could you? Instead of coming to see me, you go to a...a...place like that!" The girl stamped her foot on the board sidewalk, rage and embarrassment making her almost incoherent.

"Now Emily. You don't understand," he pleaded. "It wasn't what you think at all."

"What was it then? Was she prettier than me? Or did you prefer an older one with more experience? I understand some of them are very practiced!" A crowd was beginning to gather, attracted by the pretty girl and her obvious anger. She ignored them as she continued to rage at Frank. "We have only been engaged for three weeks. How could you do this to me just as soon as you thought I wasn't around? Is this what I have to look forward to for the rest of my life? You sneaking off to be with some evil woman?"

"Please let me explain, Emily," he implored. "Come inside where we can talk in private."

She slapped angrily at the hand he was extending towards her. "You keep your filthy hands off me, Frank Weston! Heaven only knows where they have been." She stepped back slowly shaking her head, tears in her eyes. "You stay away from me. I have to decide what I am going to do about you and I don't want to have you around while I do it."

"You tell him, honey. Don't let him sweet-talk you none. You can't never trust no man."

Emily looked around, surprised to find them the center of a circle of amused onlookers. The one who had just spoken was a frowzy, older woman carrying a string shopping bag.

She turned back to Frank, her voice quieter, but not calmer. "Just stay away from me and tell your aunt I thought better of her. No wonder everyone talks about her at home." She pushed blindly through the crowd and hurried up the street towards the Stiles house.

The crowd broke up now that the entertainment was over. Soon the only one left was the old woman. She spat, "Men!" at Frank. "They're all alike." She too stalked rightiously away.

"What was that all about?" Luther and Katherine were standing on the hotel porch above him.

Frank was confused and hurt. "Stiles told her I was at Mary Kate's place last night. I tried to explain why I was there, but she wouldn't listen."

"Good," Luther said. "The less Stiles knows the better for us. It also shows he is having us watched. He couldn't have learned about it so soon otherwise."

"What am I going to do?" Frank's voice was miserable as he stared up the street at the distant figure of the girl.

"Come inside. We have plans to make."

"It will be all right, Frank." Katherine was much more sympathetic. "When she finds out why you were there she will forgive you."

"Forgive me!" he sputtered. "The only woman I spent any time with in that place was my own aunt."

"You'll understand when you are older, Frank. Women don't think like us." Luther was grinning down at him. "She seems like a nice girl. Probably very pretty when she isn't mad about something. It should make you feel better to think about how hard she is going to have to work to make this up to you when she finally learns the truth."

Frank followed them inside, confused and miserable, his mind no longer on their problem.

"We have to have some kind of proof if we are going to get outside help. The state government isn't going to take the word of the four of us. We have to be able to substantiate every charge we make."

They had gathered in Will Karren's private rooms. The four had been trying to decide on their next move for some time. At least Luther, Katherine and Will had been, Frank's mind was elsewhere.

"But all the proof was stolen from my room," Katherine protested.

"Then we will have to steal it back." The others looked at Luther in surprise. "What other way is there?" he demanded. "The town's most important citizen and the local sheriff are behind this. Would anyone believe us if we told them? We have to collect the proof which will convince the state to act."

"What happens if we get caught?" Will asked dubiously.

"That is a good question. It is also why you won't be involved tonight. You have to stay clear in case the rest of us do get caught. We will need someone on the outside."

He thought for a moment. "Do you know someone we can trust to carry a message down to Polks for Jester?"

"Yes, I think so. When do you want him to leave?"

"As soon as I finish writing the note."

Will hurried out the back door and Luther went out to the front desk and borrowed paper and pen from the shelf under the register. He remained behind the counter leaning on the top as he concentrated on the wording of the message.

Firm footsteps crossed the lobby and he glanced up to find Benton Stiles standing only a few feet away, looking the perfect picture of a banker from hat to walking stick.

"Are you Luther North?" he demanded.

"I am," Luther replied calmly as he looked the short man up and down. "And you are?"

"Benton Stiles." There was a flash of irritation at Luther's seeming nonrecognition before he controlled it. "I wish to have a word with you."

"Here I am."

"I would prefer a more private place." Stiles looked around uncertainly.

"This is as private a place as any. No one can get close without our knowing, and Will is gone for some time on an errand."

Stiles nodded, finally. "I suppose this will have to do."

Luther watched with amusement while the small man arranged his body to give himself the most dominant appearance possible, both hands firm on the head of the cane in front of him, his tiny black eyes fixed unwaveringly on Luther's face.

"I understand," the banker began, "That you have hired out to young Weston. I think it is a mistake on your part to have done so."

"Where did you hear I've hired out, Stiles? And why would it be a mistake?" Luther grinned impudently.

"That isn't important. What is important is that Weston and his aunt are trying to cause trouble for me. They seem to have some crazy notion there is a conspiracy to steal his parent's farm. She as good as called me a thief and I won't have it."

"Are you a thief?" Luther asked with interest.

Stiles flushed. "Of course not. I am a man of standing in this community, this entire state. If she continues to go around talking in that manner I will have to take some form of action against her."

"Such as having the Sheriff's deputies beat her up in an alley like her nephew?"

"That was an unfortunate incident, which I deplore, brought on by remarks he made to those men. I don't agree with their actions, but I sympathize with them."

"I just bet you do. How about the two who tried to kill him out on the trail yesterday?"

"I thought they attacked you, not him."

"He was riding with me. They told him they were going to finish him for good. That doesn't sound like just a reaction to words to me."

"I had nothing to do with that, but..."

"But you wouldn't have been too unhappy if it had succeeded would you?" Luther was enjoying himself.

"That is an impertinence on your part. I don't like you putting words in my mouth."

"I'm the impertinant sort," Luther agreed. "Are you going to have the Sheriff's deputies come after me?"

Stiles took a deep breath to calm himself. "This had nothing to do with why I came. I want to know if you have hired out to him."

"Nope. I don't work for hire."

Stiles relaxed slightly. "I am glad to learn that."

"Of course, if anyone were to attempt to do somethng to Frank while I was around, I would find it necessary to come to his aid, just as a friendly gesture." Luther smiled pleasantly. "I'm sure you can understand that."

"Nothing is going to happen to Frank. It would be best for him to go back east where he belongs, though. He seems to have gotten off to a poor start around here."

"It is nice of you to take such an interest in his welfare."

"I am willing to forgive him for the sake of that fine girl who is staying in my home as a guest of my wife and myself."

"You are really a prince of a man, Stiles. Is there anything else you wanted?"

"No. Just your assurance that you aren't working for Weston."

"I can give you my word he isn't paying me a cent to help him. I don't work for private individuals."

The banker relaxed completely. "That answer is just what I wanted to hear."

"You have made me curious, Stiles. Is there something I would discover if I went to work for Frank?" Luther asked innocently. "You sure seem anxious for me not to do so."

"No! What could there possibly be?" Stiles asked too quickly. Then he smiled coldly, his control back. "I just want to make sure Singleshoe remains the quiet town it has always been. That is what makes it such a good place to live."

"I couldn't agree more, Stiles. I'll try not to disturb any of the honest citizens." Luther was enjoying himself.

"Good. I have to be getting back to the bank." He paused at the front door. "Good day, North. Enjoy your stay in Singleshoe."

"Don't worry," Luther called after him. "I intend to."

He finished the note and sealed it in an envelope. When he returned to the office, he found an angry Frank and a slightly confused Katherine.

"You gave him your word you weren't working for me. How could you do that?" Frank's sense of honor was more outraged than he was concerned with the banker's visit.

Katherine, on her part, eyed him cooly. "Perhaps you have an explanation."

Luther laughed which only upset them more. "I told him I wasn't working for you and I'm not."

The woman searched his face for his meaning. "I don't think I understand."

Luther sat in a chair and calmly crossed one leg over the other. "If I don't get paid, I don't see how anyone could say I am working for you."

They slowly comprehended what he was saying. Katherine said admiringly, "You are a devious man, Luther North."

Will came into the room at that moment and said, "I have a man to take that message for you, Luther." He sensed the mood in the room. "What happened?"

"Stiles was here trying to find out where I stood. I think he is a little nervous." Luther handed Will the envelope. "Make sure the man knows this is important. I want it to reach Jester as soon as possible."

Will was gone for a few minutes. When he

returned he reported, "He's off. He should be to Polks by the middle of the afternoon."

"Excellent!" Luther looked around the room at the others. "Now we can get on with planning our robbery."

"Robbery?" Frank gasped. "You were serious about stealing the papers back?"

"Of course I was. I would be willing to bet they are in Stiles' house, from what you said Emily said, Katherine. We will start there."

CHAPTER THIRTEEN

"Quick! Into those bushes," Luther whispered urgently.

They just managed to reach the badly overgrown yard of a vacant house before two men on horseback rode into view. They carried rifles openly across their saddles and their heads were constantly in motion, checking houses as they rode past. Sheriff's deputies had been riding patrol around the banker's house ever since his conversation with Luther.

The two rode slowly past where Luther, Frank

and Katherine were hidden and stopped a hundred feet away at the next corner. One threw the other a bag of makings and watched as his friend hooked a leg around his saddlehorn and began to fashion a cigarette.

"What do you suppose the boss is so worried about tonight? Don't look to me like nothing's going on." His bored voice carried clearly through the still, night air.

"It has something to do with that gunfighter down to the hotel. He's got Stiles worried, and what worries Stiles worries the boss."

"Hell. I've seen him around town before. He even bought me a drink once. Comes up to town to drink with the boys, play some poker and dip his wick over to Mary Kate's. What worries the boss about that?"

"He ain't been in a saloon since he got here to drink or play cards. And he was just over to Mary Kate's once. Took that new piece back to the hotel with him. The boss has had Banks watching him ever since he brought in Jeff Coats dead."

"I ain't all that certain that's something to hold against him. Jeff could wear on a man about as quick as anyone I ever met." He twisted the ends of the cigarette and put it between his lips, patted his shirt and vest pockets and then mumbled, "You got a light?"

A note of irritation showed in the other man's voice as he handed a match across. "You ever carry anything of your own? Give me back my makings before you forget."

"You ain't a trusting man, Harley. I don't know

why I hang around with you. If you want anything of mine, you know all you got to do is ask. I'm that kind of feller." His voice reflected his hurt feelings, but he did return the makings.

"I would think a whole lot more of that statement if you ever had anything anyone else would want."

The match flared and for a moment they had a glimpse of a worn, battered face, eyes slitted shut against the light. Harley reined his horse around impatiently, "We better get on. Stiles finds out we been sitting here talking instead of watching his house he'll have our heads."

"What's the rush? Ain't no one in that house except them two girls. He won't be back for hours."

"You can't depend on that, so I want to look like I'm working." They rode slowly out of sight, quarreling mildly.

Luther sat in the midst of the bushes and watched them melt into the darkness of the next block. He was motionless so long Frank began to fidget impatiently. "What are we waiting for? You heard those two. Stiles is out of his house. Let's get in there before he comes back. Maybe I can see Emily," he added hopefully.

"We're going to have to watch our step," Luther said softly. "I can't believe those two are the only guards around the house. Stiles is too careful a man for that." He was studying the street down which they had come.

Frank started to get up to shake the kinks out of his legs. "Keep still!" Luther ordered.

"What for?" Frank demanded. "They are gone

and there isn't another soul in sight."

"That doesn't mean there's no one out there. You heard what those two said. Stiles has someone following us. It explains how Emily knew you were at Mary Kate's last night. Whoever this Banks is, he's damn good. I haven't had a smell of him."

They waited in silence, the tension growing. Katherine finally reached out a hand and touched Luther's back just for the reassurance of the contact.

At last he murmered with satisfaction, "Got him. I want the two of you to move around and talk while I'm gone. Not loud, just enough to show there are still three people here and they are getting tired of waiting." He melted suddenly into the darkness which surrounded the deserted house.

For a few moments both stared at the spot where he had vanished. Then Katherine turned to Frank. "Tell me about your last year of school."

"Now? Whatever for?" Surprise made him raise his voice.

"Quietly," she cautioned. "Just tell me about it." Her small, firm hand grasped his wrist, "Talk, damn it!"

He finally realized what she wanted and began an animated description of the past year. She moved about a little and from time to time contributed a quiet word, all the while trying to discover what Luther had seen.

The grove of young trees down the street still had two overly thick trunks when Luther completed his circuit of the block. The man's ability to stand absolutely motionless was a marvel to Frank as he then worked his way through the tall grass which covered the vacant lot whose corner held the trees.

The breeze had picked up some during the past hour and was swaying the long grass in a series of slow rhythmical waves. The moon was partially obscured by thin clouds which didn't quite mask its light, but did provide a pattern of moving shadows across the ground. Luther used these to conceal his passage across the open field.

Finally, he lay in the heavy shadows at the edge of the grove where he could examine the watcher. Banks was small and wiry, all his attention focused at the moment on the pair of riders coming down the street.

The same two guards as before, were even more casual than on the previous round fifteen minutes earlier. Their hours of patrolling with no sign of trouble had made them careless. They saw just what they had seen before, nothing more.

Luther slowly drew his gun.

The steady rhythmic clop continued to grow in volume until the sound dominated the quiet night. When they approached the front of the grove, the watcher above him stared silently at them, unaware of the slight rustle as Luther stood.

His first indication that he wasn't alone was the strong arm snaking around his chest from behind. Even as his muscles tensed in automatic reaction, the heavy butt of the pistol descended to strike him behind the right ear, just hard enough to render him unconscious.

The strong arm held the man motionless while the patrol slowly passed. When they turned the corner and rode out of sight Luther quickly checked the condition of the man, tossed the frail body over his shoulder, and ran easily across the street to where the others waited. He led them on into the vacant house and laid the body out in a square of moonlight from one of the windows. The man was unknown to him.

Katherine handed him a handkerchief to use as a gag and removed the man's belt to bind his ankles. Frank stood to one side and watched. "Is all this really necessary?" he asked. "He won't know where we've gone and they might not find him for days. He could die all tied up like that."

Luther explained patiently, "We don't know how long he's been following us or what he's been close enough to hear. We can't take a chance on his coming to and alerting the guards while we are inside the house." Completing a knot around the man's wrists with a twisted section of the watcher's shirt, he examined Katherine's work on the ankles, nodded in satisfaction and stood.

"We can stop in here on our way back and arrange it so he can get free."

They crept silently through the house to the kitchen. From the back windows, the rear of banker Stile's house was clearly visible in the moonlight across the alley.

"Will there be any more guards?" Katherine asked.

"We have to assume so. I don't think they will be

inside the house itself, though, so once we get past them we should be safe. I'll go in first and locate them while you two wait here. Do you see that white shed?"

The two nodded. "If it is safe for you to come across I will stand there for a moment and wave. Make sure it is me before you come out."

After he opened the back door he paused for a moment. "Be careful. With all these guards there must be something very valuable in that house. Don't either of you get careless. I don't want to lose anyone."

They were able to follow his progress from shadow to shadow only because they had watched him start and knew where he was going. Then, suddenly, he disappeared.

Katherine settled back. "We will take turns watching the building. There may be only one chance to see his signal, so we will have to stay alert. Why don't you find us something to sit on." She looked at her nephew for a moment. "Be careful, Frank. If anyone should get careless, someone could die."

CHAPTER FOURTEEN

"You will walk right into him if you go on around that corner."

The voice was young, female and spoken close enough to his left ear to almost stop Luther's heart. Because of years of self-control, he was able to remain motionless. "Who are you?" he asked, when he was absolutely certain he had his voice under control.

"May Stiles. Are you here to kidnap me?" Her voice sounded hopeful.

"No." He looked at the vague outline of the young girl inside the open window. At that age, he could never tell for sure, but she looked seven or eight years old. "We just came to borrow some papers from your father's study."

She giggled. "What for? Most of them just have a lot of numbers on them. They aren't very interesting."

"Someone took them from a friend of mine and gave them to your father by mistake. She would like to have them back." Luther was unable to decide why he was talking so freely to this girl with an armed guard just around the corner.

"What's your friend's name?"

"Katherine Stone."

"That's Frank Weston's aunt, isn't it? My father said she was a bad woman. He said she was working in that house my mother won't let me walk past."

"She was hiding there from the men who stole the papers. We need them back if Frank is to keep his farm." He had a sudden inspiration, "And marry Emily."

"I don't know if I want to help Frank. He made Emily cry, and she's my friend."

"Where is Emily now?"

"Upstairs in her room. I was watching out my window when I saw you come across the yard. I knew you would come here because the window is open, so I came down to find out who you were."

The inspiration had now formed a definite plan in Luther's mind. "Do you like Emily?"

"Of course I do. She plays with me and tells me

stories. My mother won't let me play with the other children in town. She says they aren't the right sort for me to know. Emily is going to be my friend when I go back east to school next year. What did Frank do to make her cry?"

"He didn't do anything. I bet Emily started to cry right after your father talked to her, didn't she?"

"That's right. He told her Frank had been in that bad place. I was listening at the door. I do that a lot." She seemed very pleased with herself. He was gaining a picture of a lonely little girl, no friends, her only entertainment provided by what went on in the house around her. She seemed to be a bright child, though, so he decided to try to get her on their side.

"Frank was in that place, but just to meet his aunt. He didn't see any of the bad women. I would like to bring the two of them together so they can make up. Will you help me?"

"Oh, yes!" He could hear her clap her hands. "What do you want me to do?"

"They can't talk out here, the guards would chase Frank away. Can you let us into the house?"

She considered it. "My father says I'm never to let anyone in the house when he isn't here." Luther's hopes fell. "But that can't mean Frank. Besides, I don't want Emily to cry any more. Will you come with him?"

"Yes, and his Aunt Katherine. She can be the chaperone."

The girl nodded her fair head. "The man will come around the house again in a few minutes. After he passes I will unlock the side door. Should I tell

129

Emily?"

"Not until we are inside. If she gets excited it would make the guard suspicious."

"That's smart. You go and get them. I'll wait beside the door." Her outline disappeared.

As soon as the guard rounded the corner towards the front of the house, the three quickly crossed the lawn to the side door where May was waiting, almost hopping up and down in her excitement. Katherine was dressed in a tight pair of jeans and a snugly fitting shirt for the night's excursions. This costume on a woman fascinated May, so she consented to take the older woman's hand and lead them to her fatner's study.

Katherine kept her occupied while Luther went through the papers in the desk and Frank wandered the room brooding about his fiance upstairs. "How is she, May?" he asked, finally.

"She's been crying a lot. You made her very sad. That wasn't nice at all."

Luther paused in his search to read through the documents he found in a large envelope. "This looks like what we are after. You better check to see if everything is here, Katherine." She bent over the desk leaving the girl with Frank.

The door to the hall opened and Emily stood glaring at them. "Does Mr. Stiles know you are here?" she demanded in a shrill voice.

Luther grinned at her. "I sincerely hope not."

She turned on Frank. "So you've become a common thief as well as being a libertine."

130

May ran across the room and took her hand. "Come and make up with Frank. It wasn't like my father said at all."

Frank moved towards her, "You have to listen to me, Emily. I only went to that place to meet my aunt."

"I don't believe you," she said defiantly. She looked across the room at the two beside the desk. "You broke in here, didn't you?"

She suddenly screamed, followed by a loud, "Help! There are burglars in the house! Help!"

"Damn!" Luther was caught behind the desk. "Shut her up, Frank. We can't afford to be caught in here."

Emily looked Frank full in the face. "Don't you dare touch me!" Frank stood frozen, unable to move against the girl he loved, shocked by her anger. "I hate you," she continued brutally, "I hate you and never want to see you again!"

Katherine moved quickly, pushed Frank out of the way, pulled the girl inside the door and clapped her hand firmly over her mouth. The screech of the shrill voice was cut off abruptly. In the sudden silence, they could hear someone on the front porch rattling the door.

Emily squirmed violently as she tried to escape Katherine's grasp. Luther finally reached them and assumed the burden of holding on to the enraged girl. Frank made a feeble effort to protest their rough treatment.

"There's no time for that, now," Katherine snapped. "Find something to tie her up with." She looked desperately around the room.

"Get a move o: ," Luther said. "We have to get out of here before that guard finds a way in."

Katherine eyed the struggling girl speculatively then stepped across to the desk and picked up a small metal cylinder the banker used as a paperweight. "Sorry about this, Emily. Maybe someday you will actually think about what you do instead of just letting your emotions take charge."

She wrapped her fist around the cylinder. "Frank didn't come to Mary Kate's last night for a woman. If you really knew anything about him, you would realize that. He came to see me. It was the only place I could find to hide from your good banker Stiles while Frank was getting help."

Luther dropped his hand from the girl's mouth and she delivered a short, straight right to the side of Emily's jaw. The violent gasp of the air the girl was drawing in for a fresh scream was cut short.

He carried her across to a plush sofa where he laid her unconscious form out carefully. Frank knelt beside her, patting her hand and saying stupidly, "Emily, speak to me."

Luther pulled him to his feet and propelled him across the room towards the door. "Get a grip on yourself, Frank," his aunt ordered sharply. "She'll be all right and we have to get out of here." Luther towed him down the hall towards the side door.

Katherine bent over the little girl, "You stay with her, May. Tell her I'm sorry I had to hit her, but there wasn't time to argue any longer. Don't worry about her; she'll be all right in a few minutes."

May nodded soberly and went to sit on the edge of the sofa and hold Emily's hand. Katherine ran down the hall and slipped through the door into the night. Luther reached out a hand from the deep shadow under a tree and pulled her in beside him. A man ran across the lawn carrying his rifle at the ready. He tried the side door, found it unlocked and disappeared inside.

She didn't protest the comfort of the protective arm he kept around her. "Remind me not to get in any fights with you," he said admiringly. "Where did you learn that trick?"

"One of the hands showed it to me when I was working on a steamboat out of St. Louis. He said it would protect my knuckles and give me the force to deck a big drunk. That and the fact a man never expects it from a woman were what I needed." She hesitated. "I tried to hold back. You don't think I hit her too hard, do you?"

"It was just right," he assured her?"

He had been keeping an eye on the neighborhood. "They all seem to be inside. Let's get out of here while we can."

CHAPTER FIFTEEN

The town was alive with armed riders. They quartered the neighborhood calling to one another, searching in every possible hiding place. The noise they were making was awakening the people of the town, so lights were appearing here and there and making it difficult for the three fugitives to find a spot in which to hide.

For a moment they lay in the tall grass of the same vacant lot Luther had crossed to reach the watcher earlier. He fished in the front of his shirt for the envelope he had taken from Stiles' desk and slid it across to Katherine. "You better carry this. They can't very well accuse you of stealing it."

She folded the envelope and thrust it securely inside her belt. "What are we going to do now, Luther? We won't be able to get back to the hotel, not with all this going on."

"We'll wait until it calms down some and then find a way out to Frank's farm. Your brother was a man who planned ahead, I bet he had supplies stored out there in case of an emergency. Once we are safe we can plan our next step."

He lay on his back and looked up at the bright stars, blotted here and there by rapidly moving clouds. "There may be some gunplay. If there is, I want you to get Frank away to the farm so I won't have to worry about you."

"I couldn't leave you alone," she said determinedly.

"You will if I tell you to. When the moment comes, there won't be time for us to argue it. Up to now you've shown a lot of sense. You know I won't ask you to do anything that isn't necessary. I just won't be able to function as well as I will have to if I am worried about you."

She reached across and took his hand. "You won't have to worry about us. I'll do whatever you say."

He squeezed the hand. "I had a feeling I could count on you."

The clouds finally obscured the moon and most of the stars. It was as dark as it was going to get. Luther sat up and looked around the new quiet neighborhood. The noise of the search had moved towards the business section, concentrating around the hotel. "Let's go. Frank, you stay close behind me. Katherine, keep a watch behind us." They moved across the open lot into the darkness beside a small stable.

It took them a long time to find a way through the patrolling men to Luther's objective. When they finally arrived, he posted Katherine where she could keep an eye on the street while he worked his way through the corrals to the livery barn. He left Frank sitting against a fence post, unable to think about anything except Emily. The boy was worse than useless.

His wagon was missing from the cluttered yard. The door to the barn gaped open, its black maw inviting him inside. He stood for a moment while he inserted a cartridge in the empty chamber he had been carrying under the hammer and studied the interior.

Then he walked right in the door.

He could feel the muscles in his neck and back tense as he passed inside, expecting at any moment the violent impact of the first slug.

Silence.

He stood next to one of the thick columns beside the wide aisle which ran between the stalls from the front to the back door while he carefully looked around. The team for his wagon was also missing.

A motion at the front of the barn solidified to become a man carrying a shotgun. "You've already looked at everything here," the man said. "Ain't nobody hiding out in my barn."

"What happened to my wagon and team?" Luther asked the man.

The shadow approached so he could see better. "That you, Luther?" His voice dropped suddenly and he looked around to make sure they were alone. "You shouldn't be here. The Sheriff has his men out turning the town upside down looking for you and that Weston boy. Says you broke into the banker's house and attacked a woman guest." His voice took on a shade of curiosity. "Did you do that, Luther?"

"We didn't break in and the guest was Weston's girl. He wanted to talk to her. Stiles didn't want him to, for some reason."

"That man has real devious ways. Can't never tell just what he is thinking." He lowered his voice even more. "You better be careful, Luther. The men who were in here earlier ain't going to be too backward about shooting you if they should get the chance."

"I know. We've run across several of them already. What happened to the team and wagon I left here yesterday?" His impatience with the man was close to the surface.

"Will Karren came by a couple of hours ago, back before the town got all stirred up. Took it and loaded it with stuff from his hotel. Last I saw he was headed west across the tracks." He suddenly looked concerned. "Will said it would be all right with you. Did I do wrong to let him have it?"

"You did just right. Does the Sheriff know about it?"

"Don't see how. He didn't say nothing to me

about it, so I didn't see no reason to bring it up."

"Thanks, Cam. Why don't you turn in now. I wouldn't want them to find you standing here like something was going on."

Cam chuckled. "I guess I could use the sleep." He started back towards his room and then turned. "One other thing, Luther. There are three saddled horses tied to that rack up on the side street runs along the hotel."

Luther regarded him with interest, "And?"

"There's a man at a window on the second floor of the hotel and another on the roof across the street. Them's the only three horses out on the street that don't seem to be watched."

"I owe you, Cam, and I won't forget."

The man grunted, pleased. "I'd like to see the town get back to what it was before he got so damned greedy."

"You stay out of it, Cam. I don't want any honest folk to get hurt."

Luther stood for a moment just inside the front door watching the activity up the street. The searchers seemed to be drawing back. Two of them rode past, taking the road west across the tracks.

A wave to Katherine where she watched from the darkness under the wooden awning of the blacksmith's, and they met back beside Frank at the corral. "We have to draw them away from the road west. Will told me earlier if things got too hot around town he would meet us at one of the abandoned farms, just a couple of miles west of town. I'm going to give the Sheriff and his men something else to think about so you two can get out of here."

He pointed to a dark building beside the tracks. "That's the farmers's marketing association warehouse. Wait over beside it until the shooting starts. When those two riders who passed a few minutes ago come back in, I want the two of you to get out with Will."

"We can't just go off and leave you," Katherine protested.

"Remember, I said you would have to trust me when I told you to do something. I can take care of myself, so please do as I say. With you out of town I can consider anyone I meet an enemy."

She stood on her toes and kissed him full on the lips. "You be careful, Luther North. I'm growing very fond of you." After hugging him for a moment she stepped back slightly. "Do you want us to wait where Will is until you get there?"

He shook his head. "Go on out to Frank's farm. I'll be there by daylight." His hands held her momentarily. "Keep a good watch. You and I have a few things to discuss when this is over."

She led a still bemused Frank towards the warehouse.

Luther lay motionless under the board sidewalk Main. They had set a trap for him with those three horses as bait. A trap discovered could often be turned to the intended victim's advantage. He intended this to be one of those times.

Luther lay motionless under the board sidewalk across Main from the hotel. The three horses down the side street were clearly visible, and he had located the man on the roof. Twice now he had shifted positions hoping to discover the position of the man in the hotel. Not for a moment did he consider the information Cam had given him might be incorrect.

A match finally flared behind the third window from the corner. From time to time then as he waited, he could see a red glow as the man drew on his cigarette.

He rolled out from under the sidewalk and stood in the doorway of a shop. Two mounted men rode past, the same pair he had seen ride out earlier towards the west. That solved one of his problems. He waited until they reached Sailor's Saloon where the Sheriff's men had established their headquarters. In the time he had been watching, the increased noise level showed a considerable consumption of the bar's whiskey.

Adjusting his hat with both hands in order to shield his face from anyone who might be watching, he crossed Main and walked down the side street towards the horses, keeping close to the wall of the hotel so he would be out of sight of the man in the room on the second floor. The small bulge in the skyline, which was the man on the roof changed shape continually as he moved to keep Luther in view.

The horses stood hitched to the rack, heads drooping, resting on three legs, as they patiently awaited whatever was in store. Something about them seemed just a little wrong, so he stopped to examine them more carefully.

He chuckled suddenly in admiration. They were too damned comfortable. Their saddle cinches had been loosened. Anyone who made a quick attempt to mount would find himself in a heap on the ground, an easy target for the watching gunmen.

When he finally moved towards the horses, he ducked under the rack and came up between the center and left-hand animals. The bulge on the roof expanded to become a man's upper body.

Luther remaimed hunched over so his head wouldn't show above the saddles and give the rifle-man a target while he tightened the cinch.

This didn't deter the man on the roof. The first shot he triggered slammed into the wall of the hotel after passing just above the heads of the horses. The explosion echoed between the buildings, bringing a cascade of falling sparks as the startled man in the hotel dropped his cigarette out the window and grabbed for his gun.

The saddle secure, Luther untied the reins of all three horses and held them in his left hand as he took careful aim at the man on the roof. The first shot went home and the bulge disappeared from view, swearing harshly.

His second shot shattered the glass in the window above him, forcing the man there to pull his head back inside.

Stepping into the saddle, he yelled a fierce, defiant cry and fired twice more at the window. The other two horses fled the scene, one with its loose saddle slowly turning to bump along under its stomach. The one he was riding pitched wildly a couple of times with the excitement and then responded to the drumming of his heels to gallop down the side street towards the road south.

Luther continued on for two blocks making as much noise as possible. He could hear the uproar as men poured out of Sailor's in response to the shooting at the hotel.

He took the next corner to the right, slowing so the animal made little noise on the sandy street. Another two blocks and he turned right again, riding to the corner with Main Street. Reining in the horse he surveyed the scene in front of Sailor's while he reloaded his revolver.

The Sheriff's men were a bit the worse for their time in the saloon. The street was a confusion of horses trying to avoid the men stumbling around under their hooves. Their riders were jerking at saddlehorn and reins in an attempt to mount and get to the scene of the ambush. They were all calling loudly and swearing impressively in whiskey slurred voices.

Luther rode slowly down the street and, with his hat pulled well down over his eyes, joined the disorganized mob.

Sheriff Carr finally got them moving and they set off down the street in a jostling mass. The two riderless horses were just visible across the railroad tracks.

"Somebody get after those animals," the Sheriff ordered.

With a wave of his arm Luther slowly rode across the tracks towards the horses. None of the other riders were interested. They were all anxious to get on down the road south after the man who had sprung the trap.

After Luther caught the horses he took the time to secure their saddles properly and, finding no one was paying the slightest bit of attention to him, set off along the road to the west.

CHAPTER SIXTEEN

The midmorning heat awakened Luther, the mouldy, bitter taste in his mouth adding spice to a slight headache. He rolled up to sit on the edge of the horsehair sofa and, with almost sensual pleasure, rubbed the sleep from his eyes with his hands. Across the room Will Karren slept soundly and noisily on his back under the open front windows, the gusty exhaust of his snoring tossing the ends of his mustache wildly.

Luther shuffled into the kitchen, carrying his

boots, not quite able to supress a huge yawn. He bent and stretched as he moved, attempting to work out the aches and pains which a night on the uncomfortable couch had produced.

He pumped the kitchen basin full of cold water and buried his face to the ears, letting the cold soak the tiredness away. When he emerged, sputtering, Katherine was there to hand him a towel.

She looked fresh and clean and a bit amused by his appearance. "If you want to shave there is hot water in the range reservoir and soap and a razor on the back porch. I'll have your breakfast ready when you're finished."

"Where's Frank?" he mumbled as he walked out onto the sunny porch.

"I sent him up on the hill behind the house to keep watch. I thought it would be a good idea if we had advance warning of anyone who tried to approach, and you and Will worked too hard last night to be disturbed. Besides," she sighed, "I couldn't stand much more of his moping around the house about Emily. I hope time to think, with no one else around, will help him clear his head."

By the time he finished wiping the last of the lather from behind his ears, she had breakfast on the table, and he fell to with a huge appetite. It gave him a chance to think over last night after escaping from the town.

He had come across country, being careful to leave no trail so as not to lead Carr and Stiles to them too quickly. Even with the care he had taken he had arrived at the farm before the three on the wagon.

Frank had wandered around his parent's last home looking at pictures and suffering morbidly while he and Will had worked into the dawn getting the house ready for whatever might come next. He had sent Katherine to bed early so there would be someone alert this morning. Finally, as ready as they could get, he and Will had tossed to see who would sleep on the sofa in the front room and who would have to drag a mattress down from upstairs. He had won the toss and made the wrong choice.

The snoring in the front room cut off abruptly with a strangled snort, and they could hear Will muttering as he snored himself awake. He came into the kitchen and slumped into a chair at the table where a cup of coffee revived him enough to ask Katherine, "How did your little set-to with Frank this morning end up? I didn't hear the end of it."

She looked at him with surprise. "I didn't realize anyone else heard that." For some reason she didn't seem pleased.

Luther asked, "Something happened this morning?"

"I was on my way back from the privy and I heard them arguing. You really set him straight, Katherine."

"What was it?" Her reluctance to talk about it was making him curious.

"Frank wanted to go back to town," she said finally. "He wanted to tell Stiles he wouldn't fight over the farm and the rest of us would leave town."

"I didn't hear that part," Will said. "What does he

expect me to do with my hotel? Donate it to Stiles and his crooked friends?"

Katherine laid a hand on his shoulder. "He isn't thinking very clearly, Will. The only thing on his mind at the moment is Emily. The last thing she said to him was she hated him and never wanted to see him again. He would do anything to fix it up between them again."

Luther stood suddenly, knocking over his chair. He started for the front room. "And you left him out there on guard?" He pushed through the front door, buckling on his gunbelt as he ran across the yard towards the hill which overlooked the farm and most of the surrounding countryside.

The side nearest the house was unclimbable so he ran through the brush at its base and circled the hill to the less abrupt western face. There were two strange horses tethered to a bush.

Katherine and Will ran up behind him. "Oh damn!" she blurted. "I should have known better than to send him out here alone."

"He may have just been brooding about Emily and they caught him off guard. It doesn't mean he let them climb the hill without warning us." He looked at Katherine. "I want you to take these horses back to the farm and then watch the hill from the front porch. Will, you set up on that rise over there with your rifle. You should be able to make sure that anyone who is on that hill stays there."

"What are you going to do, Luther? I don't want Frank hurt." Katherine's eyes were pleading with him.

"I'm going to go up that hill and get Frank back, whether he wants it or not. Both of you be certain of your targets before you fire at anyone. Remember, half the people on that hill are supposed to be on our side."

Katherine led the horses around the base of the hill and across the wide farm yard which caused consternation near the crest of the hill. Luther could hear them moving around and calling back and forth. Will settled into a hollow concealed by a healthy growth of late spring grass and waved he was ready.

Luther moved around the hill to the southern approach. The only worn path to the crest ran up the western side. He hoped they would be paying more attention to it than the rest of the hill.

It took him the better part of fifteen minutes to work his way three-quarters up the hill. From time to time he could see movement among the jumble of rocks which covered the crest.

A man in a red shirt stepped into view facing more to the west than Luther's position. "You hold it, North!" the man shouted. "We got young Weston up here. If you don't want him killed, you'll bring our horses back and another for him so we can ride out of here. You're working for him and that's what he wants you to do."

From where Luther crouched it was an almost impossible shot at the man. He would have to shift a few feet to his right if he wanted to stay under cover. Or stand up if he didn't.

He stood to find Frank between him and his

target. "Get out of the way, Frank!" he yelled.

Both men turned to look at him in surprise. "No, Luther," the boy called. "I want you to do as he says. I have to see Emily and try to explain all this to her. The farm isn't that important to me anymore."

The morning sun glinted from metal in the rocks above the two. Luther dropped in his tracks and the bullet whined past into the distance. From his position below, Will placed three careful shots into the rocks around the gunmen and drove him to cover.

Luther took advantage of this to scramble across several yards of open ground to a large boulder which would shelter him from the men above. He moved on around it to find himself at the edge of the vertical eastern face of the hill looking down into the farm yard. Katherine stood, rifle in hand, on the porch, eyes searching the hill. He waved to show her his position and saw her recognition, though she made no move which would reveal him to the two men above.

Continuing on around the rock he found himself confronted with a narrow ledge which crossed the almost sheer rock face of the hill. There appeared to be a patch of brush at the other end which he could use for cover to reach the summit if he could get that far safely.

He had no choice but to cross the ledge. The other side of the boulder was in plain view of the men above. The ledge itself was narrow, but would be no real problem. About three-quarters of the way across, however, the remains of a dying bush thrust a tangle of branches across the path. He would have to find a way around or under it.

It was only a moment's run across to the bush. There, however, he was presented with more of a problem than he had thought from the side. Dead branches were mixed with just enough gnarled living ones to make it impossible for him to break them all off with his hands. He knelt and began to snap off the dead wood near the bottom. Soon all were clear except for one limber branch which was far enough on the other side of the bush he couldn't get the leverage he needed to break it. There was a chance if he held it up he might be able to crawl under it.

Lying on his back he propelled himself slowly along with his shoulderblades and feet. Progress was slow and the remaining branches above clutched at him like a lot of great, sticky fingers. He had to reholster his gun in order to use both hands to lift the living branch out of the way, and he was feeling very naked and exposed.

The branch proved to be very stubborn. Using both hands he finally forced it up just enough for him to slowly begin to slide under. His upper body was just clear when a shot rang out from the farmyard below.

He looked down in surprise and the branch slipped out of his hand to pin him against the ledge. Katherine gestured towards the brush at the end of the ledge. He twisted around until he could look over his shoulder and saw a man working his way down to where he would have a clear shot at him.

Luther attempted to roll up on his left side so his

holster would be accessible. The branches entangled themselves with his belt. He wrenched at it desperately, forgetting for a moment just how narrow the ledge was.

He drew the gun as he continued to thrash around in an attempt to find a position from which he could see the man clearly. It would be impossible to fire at him while lying on his back and over his shoulder. He had to get free of the branches.

A final desperate jerk on his belt succeeded in separating him from the bush.

But the sudden release overbalanced him and before he could recover he tumbled over the rim of the ledge.

His left arm flailed desperately as the support went out from under him, his searching fingers coming in contact with the same branch which had caused him the trouble in the first place. While his hand scrabbled for a hold on the gnarled wood, the gunman stepped into plain view at the end of the path, a smile of anticipation growing on his face as he saw Luther's predicament.

Luther had been waving his gun-filled right hand around as a counterbalance to his left. It was now about chest high and extending out along the rock face.

He pushed a few inches away from the surface with his knees, took desperate aim and shot the man in the chest.

As he was suspended by his left hand from the branch directly above, he pivoted outwards in reaction to the recoil of the pistol. A wrenching turn of his wrist stopped the motion and he slowly swung back to where he could see the man again.

The look of anticipation on the man's face had been replaced by one of surprise. His gun was forgotten in his right hand as his left slowly reached up to examine the hole in his chest from which frothy blood was beginning to bubble.

Luther struggled to again raise the pistol towards the man, but the wild gyrations as he swung and pivoted from the branch above prevented it.

His foot struck the rock, face beneath him and again spun him around. As he turned he heard the man's gun strike the ledge and bounce away into space. He managed to counter the latest swing just in time to see the man, both hands now grasping at his chest, slowly fold over the edge into space.

The body bounced three times before it snagged for a moment on a bush far below which was strong enough to retard its violent plunge, but not to stop it entirely. The last of its momentum twisted the body free and it rolled into the brush at the foot of the hill.

Luther stared at it for a moment and then across at Katherine. She reluctantly left the shelter of the porch and came across the yard to examine the body. Then she stood and shook her head.

When he carefully replaced the revolver in its holster he sensed for the first time a slight give in the branch from which he was suspeneded. He turned carefully until he was spread-eagle against the face of the cliff, left arm extended straight up to the branch, his right hand cautiously creeping upwards across the rock face, searching for a hold on the edge of the ledge. When his fingers reached firm ground he began to grope with the toe of his right boot for any usable projection on the rock below.

It finally located a small knob of rock. He carefully shifted his weight to his right side and took the strain off the branch. As he did, a slight trickle of dirt fell on his left shoulder from the crack out of which the bush grew. It wouldn't take much more to pull the bush free.

Secure for the moment, he looked down and located another projection to the right of the one his foot was on and several inches higher. Slowly he inched his right hand along the rim slid his left foot onto the bump beside his right.

Very slowly he released the bush completely with his left hand and dropped it to grasp the ledge. It slipped for a few inches across the smooth surface before it found a tentative grip. Careful not to make any sudden moves which would upset his center of balance against the wall, he shifted his weight from his right to his left foot. When he again felt secure he began to search with his right toe for the new foothold.

He couldn't find it!

He had to turn his head and pull out from the rock face slightly in order to look under his right arm. That meant more of his weight hung from his fingers and less was supported by his foot. Gravity began to pull him away from the cliff. His only hope was that his fingers could stand the strain long enough for him to find the new foothold.

The projection was about six inches farther over

than he had thought.

He shifted his entire body in that direction.

His left hand began to slip from its very tentative grip on the ledge. Nothing he could do would prevent it. When he had leaned back to look for the projection, the friction which gave his fingers their grip on the smooth surface had been reduced just enough to make the difference.

What seemed like hours slipped past as the fingers slowly slid along the surface of the ledge until only the length from the first joint to the tips remained in contact.

He could no longer afford to play it safe.

He shifted his entire weight onto his right foot.

A strong thrust with his left foot and a corresponding pull with his right hand started him in an upward arc across the face of the cliff. An instant later he thrust with all the strength in his right leg to throw himself up towards the ledge. His left arm to the shoulder fell across the ledge and his left knee just caught the edge.

A small projection appeared under his right hand and he pushed desperately, throwing himself up and over the rim of the ledge to lie on his back, panting heavily, sweat running into his eyes. It took him several minutes to control his ragged breathing and wildly pumping heart. Finally, calmer, he reached down to make sure he still had his gun and sat up on the ledge.

Below him, Katherine still stood beside the body of the man he had shot, watching anxiously for his reappearance. He grinned weakly and waved her back towards the shelter of the porch. The tension went out of her body when he signaled and she obeyed gladly.

He crawled along the remainder of the ledge to the safety of the bushes where he slumped into shelter and waited for the shaking of his strained muscles to stop. Only then did he turn to the problem of the remaining man.

There was a path of sorts leading upward towards the jumble of rocks, and he followed it, reloaded revolver ready in his hand. Near the crest of the hill he peered around the edge of a boulder to find Frank staring back at him. The boy's eyes widened in surprise at his sudden appearance and he started to say something. Luther shook his head and mouthed silently, "Where is he?"

Frank inclined his head to his left and said out loud, "Over there."

Luther came around the rock just as the man in the red shirt turned from examining the brush where Will was concealed. "You see anything back there, Frank? That gunshot sounded like he might have finished North."

"Not quite," Luther said softly.

The man's mouth dropped open, and he swung his revolver up, thumbing back the hammer.

Luther shot him in the right shoulder and the gun dropped unfired from his hand.

Frank started forward to pick it up, but Luther put out a hand to stop him. "Leave it."

He examined the man's shoulder, tore a square patch from the red shirt for him to hold over the wound and yelled down the hill for Will to join them. When he did, Luther said, "Stay up here and keep your eyes open. I want to have a few words with Frank in private."

"I expect you do," Will replied knowingly. He looked at Luther's torn clothing and scraped hands and arms. "You look like you fell off a cliff."

Luther laughed, "That is just what I did. I'll tell you about it later. Right now I want to get this man down to the house and see if I can learn anything about Stiles' plans."

Will nodded. "No need to worry about me. I'll be all right up here. Send me up something to drink later and I should be good for the whole day."

"You see anyone coming, you get right down to the house. I don't want you trapped up here. Katherine and I would have a hard time holding that house alone."

"What about Frank?" Will asked in surprise.

"I'm not sure he is going to help." Luther's voice was calm, but disgusted. "When I came up the last part of the hill, he was keeping watch for this punk."

He pointed the way down the hill, waited for Frank to slip an arm around the wounded man's waist so he could help him over the rough spots, and followed them towards the house.

CHAPTER SEVENTEEN

Katherine worked on his many scrapes and cuts while Luther told her of the capture. While they talked Frank sat sullenly across the kitchen table from them, staring at his hands.

"I can't believe he actually was helping them, Luther. That is ridiculous!" She looked across at her nephew. "Tell him it isn't true, Frank."

"Can't either of you understand? I want to go back to town. I have to see Emily. Nothing else matters any more." His voice was defiant.

As her anger increased, Katherine rubbed harder on Luther's abrasions. She asked Frank, coldly, "What about Will Karren? He is risking everything to help you. He can't go back while Stiles and the Sheriff control Singleshoe. What about Luther? He's had to kill for you. Doesn't that mean anything to you?"

"I don't care about any of that. I didn't ask Karren to help me. I only want to make it up with Emily." His voice remained defiant, but her anger was frightening him.

She dropped the cloth in the pan of water and turned on him. Luther removed himself from the table with considerable relief and finished patching himself up at the counter beside the pump while she stalked around the kitchen in a rage.

"You don't care that because he was willing to help you, Will could lose his business or his life? If he hadn't stopped those men from beating you in the alley and given you a place to hide, you might be dead now. What kind of person are you? You can't be the son of my brother!"

She was advancing on him with the obvious intention of doing severe bodily harm when boots pounded across the wooden porch and Will burst into the room.

"There is a rider coming fast, followed by maybe ten or twelve more. They're just a couple of minutes away," he finished, gasping for breath after his long run down from the hill.

Luther sprinted through the house grabbing his rifle from the small table beside the front door. He found a position behind one of the porch pillars and waited for Will's rider to come into view. The hotel-keeper's rifle barrel poked out the parlor bay window in support. From there he had a good view of the approach to the house across the open fields.

The house was a hundred feet from the base of the hill with only a fringe of brush to provide cover on that side. A plot of grass with a picket fence formed the front yard on the south and continued on around to the east side of the house. Its low fence was at the most, ten yards from the house.

The hard-packed dirt of the farmyard extended away on three sides. Two hundred yards to the south was the fence which ran along the road to Single-shoe. The burned-out shell of the barn, the mound of the potato cellar and several outbuildings formed a line about fifty yards to the east. Beyond that a large pasture ran down to the stream in the distance. To the north were several more small buildings, the closest about fifty yards from the house.

To reach the house any attacker would have to cross at least fifty yards of open ground and then climb the picket fence. It was a defensible position if they remained alert.

Katherine asked from the darkness of the door behind him. "Can you see who it is yet?" They stared at the plume of dust rising into the clear sky.

Luther shook his head, "Not until he comes up over that small rise. It shields the lower valley from us."

The horse galloped into view over the hill, its small rider hanging on for dear life. Something was flapping wildly along the animal's side which Luther couldn't figure out for a moment. Then he realized it was a skirt. "I think it's a girl," he said.

Katherine came out to stand beside him. "It's Emily. What do you suppose she wants."

"If she has the same backbone as Frank she probably wants us to give up so she can be a hero to the local banker."

"Don't you talk that way about Emily! I won't stand for it." Frank had followed his aunt out on the porch.

Luther was watching the heavier plume of dust which was engulfing the girl's. The large body of riders was close behind her. "What you want doesn't matter much any more," he said absently.

The girl rushed into the yard. "The Sheriff and his men are right behind me," she called as she jerked the sweat-lathered horse to a stop.

Luther didn't leave the porch. "Nice of you to bring them right to us, Miss Johnstone." His voice was heavy with irony.

She gaped at him with surprise as Frank ran out to help her dismount. "I don't understand. I heard Mr. Stiles and the Sheriff planning on coming out here. They said something about things had to be finished now. I thought you would want to know." Her voice slowly died away under his cold glare.

The silence ran on for several moments until it was almost unbearable in its intensity. The girl watched them in growing puzzlement. "What do you plan to do now, Emily?" Katherine asked.

The girl was confused. "I was going to stay here

and help." She looked from one to the other, not missing Will leaning from the parlor window, rifle in hand. "If you don't want me to stay," she began miserably.

Luther stalked down the steps and slapped her horse on the rump with his hand. The tired animal only trotted as far as the water trough beside the barn. "I had about all your help I could stand last night at the Stile's house. What was it you intend to do for us this time?"

The sudden blush was apparent even on a face flushed by the hard ride. She looked at the ground for a moment and then reached out a hand to Frank. "I don't know how I could have said or done the things I did last night. You have to know I would never hurt you, Frank. I love you."

"You better get under cover," Will interrupted. "We are about to have company."

Luther looked up to discover the Sheriff and his men only a hundred yards from the gate and coming hard. He took Emily and Frank firmly by the arm and hustled them up onto the porch. "Katherine," he ordered. "Get them under cover."

As the gang thundered into the yard he jacked a shell into the chamber of his rifle and shot the hat from Sheriff Carr's head. The men slid to a sudden halt in a mass of pitching, scrambling horses.

Luther waited for them to quiet and said, "You better have a damn good reason for being here, Henry. I would hate to kill you before the legislature had a chance to take away your job."

Carr sat for a moment, his long grey hair tossed

by his wild ride. "I'm the legal law officer in this county, North. You are obliged to do as I say."

"I don't feel at all obliged," Luther retorted calmly.

The Sheriff was purposely keeping his eyes away from the hill which overlooked the yard. It suddenly dawned on Luther that the two men who had come to the hill earlier hadn't come as scouts. Carr already knew as much as he needed to about the layout of the farm. He had wanted a couple of good riflemen on that commanding position before he arrived.

One of the gang chased down the Sheriff's hat, the spotless white felt now marred by a round hole in the crown.

Henry distastefully stuck a finger through it and then urged his horse a bit closer to Luther. "What can you gain from a fight, Luther? This farm is the legal property of the bank. You have no right to be here and I've come to put you off. There will be a lot of trouble for you if you resist the law."

"I had a look at that loan agreement last night while I was in the banker's house collecting some other papers which seemed to have wandered in there, papers belonging to Miss Stone. The next payment on that loan isn't due for another two weeks. You and Stiles were probably afraid to set the due date too close to when you killed Weston. The bank has no reason to foreclose on this property. Besides, my friends want a court to have a look at that paper. There seems to be some doubt it is valid."

"What do you mean?" Carr blustered. "I was

there when Franklin Weston signed it."

Luther was surprised to hear Frank speak up from the porch. "I can prove it isn't my father's signature. That will make both you and Stiles liable for embezzlement."

The Sheriff made one last attempt to give what was about to happen, the cloak of legality. "You all broke into Benton Stiles' house last night and assaulted a guest of his while you stole those papers."

"We will be glad to produce the papers we took in a court of law, Henry. Perhaps Stiles will have some explanation as to why they were in his house after being stolen from the rightful owner. Also, you might want to talk to May Stiles. She let us in the house. We didn't break in."

"And no one assaulted anyone. You have to have a victim, and I don't think she is agreeable." Emily stepped into view on the porch beside Frank.

"Then so be it, Luther." The Sheriff smiled down at him, a look of evil pleasure on his face. "You got in with the wrong crowd this time. You should have stuck to government work."

He raised his hat and waved it back and forth in a wide arc above his head. The look of surprise which washed over his face when nothing happened almost brought a deep laugh from Luther. The Sheriff waved again, desperation beginning to show in his manner. The men behind him began to move around nervously.

Luther slowly raised his rifle until it pointed directly at the man in his colorful costume. "You tell your men to keep still, Henry. If I get excited, I'm liable to shoot you so I can get to them."

A sharp word from Carr quieted his men. They were all covertly studying the crest of the hill above them. The Sheriff seemed about to wave the hat again.

"Don't bother to signal any more, Henry," Luther said. "There's no one up there. One is locked in the shed out back with a busted shoulder." He looked around, "Fetch him, Will. He's no use to them and just a bother to us."

The men in the gang began to stir again. Luther swung his rifle in their direction. "If you send a couple of men over to that brush at the foot of the hill, they'll find the other one. Get him off the property, too. We don't like dead scum lying around."

The man in the red shirt, a darker patch now caked on the right shoulder and a white bandage showing across his chest, stumbled around the corner followed by a grinning Will Karren.

"I think this is one of your gutter rats, Henry," he said, enjoying himself immensely.

"You know you are finished in Singleshoe, don't you Karren?" the Sheriff growled. "You best leave the country while you still can."

"I'm just getting started in Singleshoe, Henry. I'm going to be a very important man when you're gone. Can't you see the writing on the wall?"

"I will be around a long time yet," the Sheriff blustered fiercely. "There are a lot of things I haven't finished and people I want to pay back."

Will had remained by the corner of the house, so

he wouldn't be close enough to Luther for the gang to concentrate their fire in one direction. He spoke calmly, "You were a good man once, Henry. A bit pompous and showboaty, but a man who did his job well enough to keep the voters happy. What changed you?"

For a moment the stone facade cracked and the Sheriff's true feelings were revealed. "You know what the county pays me, Will. No man can live right on that."

Will shook his head. "That isn't a good enough reason, Henry. You make more money than three-quarters of the men in this county. You had a job for life, if you were careful which didn't require you to work very hard. The only thing you are saying is greed got the better part of you."

Sheriff Carr frowned. "It doesn't make much difference now, does it? It all comes down to, I can't let you get away from here alive. You know that as well as I do."

Luther said softly, "You could take a chance on the courts, Henry. Turn state's evidence against Stiles. There's no reason for more killing."

Carr laughed hollowly, "They would find me guilty in a minute, Luther. Juries don't like lawmen who use their offices to get rich. No, if I'm going to come out of this I have to fix it so there won't be any witnesses left against me. There is nothing more to say."

"I'm sorry then, Henry. You might just as well have your men take that body. I don't want it around. Their horses are tied over there where the

165

barn was before you burned it."

They stood watching each other while a couple of the gang fetched the horses, loaded the body and assisted the red shirted man to mount. When they were about to ride out Luther stopped them.

"You should know I sent a message to Denver, Henry. You have, at the most, twenty-four hours to get out of the state. If I were one of your men I wouldn't waste my time hanging around here."

"Nonsense," Henry blurted. "There was no way you could send a message. You didn't go near the telegraph or the post office." He jerked his horse around and spurred it viciously, making it leap into motion.

As the dust from the horses swirled across the yard, Luther stepped up on the porch and chased the others inside. They were just in time. Under cover of the cloud of dust, a volley of bullets swept the area where they had been standing.

Will used the time to climb to a second floor-window where he could be seen over the dust and inflict some damage on the retreating men. Luther contributed a few shots from below to show he hadn't been put out of commision either.

Then, suddenly, all was quiet. The gang began to set up a camp just outside of gunshot of the house.

Frank grabbed his arm as Luther started for the stairs. "Why didn't you shoot him while you had him cold?"

He looked at the intense boy and said with disgust. "There were a dozen men behind him. If I had shot him, they would have cut me to ribbons. I don't like you well enough to die like that for you." He slowly climbed the steps to join Will on the second floor where he could survey the layout of the besieging gang.

"Why don't you grow up?" Katherine snapped angrily. "He and Will are risking everything for you. Give them some help for a change."

CHAPTER EIGHTEEN

"There is something moving in the pasture, Mr. North!"

Luther ran through the dark room to the window beside which Emily crouched, rifle in hand. They had nailed shut or barricaded what windows they could, leaving only the few from which their fire could command all the approaches to the building.

But there were only five of them. A concerted rush on all four sides would prove almost impossible for them to stop. Katherine and Will were good with a gun and could be left alone. Frank was almost useless, but Emily had a determined manner about her that Luther liked, now that she had decided which side she was on. He had put them together hoping her nerve would steady Frank's. He had stationed himself in the next room in order to be able to help them when the time came.

In the light of the early evening moon he could see the movement she had spotted beyond the burned-out barn. "Frank. Go tell Will and your aunt they are moving in, for them to stay alert." The boy shuffled out of the room.

He checked again on his side. Nothing was moving. When he returned to Emily's window, he could identify four shadows working slowly towards the house. "You go watch on my side. I'll stay here for now."

She stepped back to give him room. "What's happened to Frank? He used to be so confidant of himself. Now he just kind of wanders."

"A combination of things, I suppose." He was watching one of the men who was working his way across the open ground towards the shelter of the horse trough. "He's young. When his family was killed and he found the men who were responsible weren't being punished he got mad and came for me. Then he returned here only to have the girl he loves turn on him. It confused him. All he had left that mattered to him was on the other side."

The man rose from shelter behind the blackened hump of the burned-out barn wall and began to scuttle across the open ground. Luther waited until he was out of reach of any shelter and dropped him with a single shot. The man lay moaning loudly in a clear patch of moonlight.

"Then it is my fault. Is that what you are saying?"

"Partly, and partly the way he looks at himself. There's nothing we are doing at the moment he is any good at." One of the wounded man's friends was crawling slowly across the open ground towards him. "He can't use a gun well, or fight with his fists. They proved that to him when they beat him in that alley. He needs to find something he can contribute to his own cause."

"What can he do?" she asked doubtfully.

"I don't have the slightest idea. We will just have to see if we can put him in a position where something he does helps the rest of us."

Luther shot the second man just before he reached his friend. He turned to look at the girl standing in the door. "You get on into the other room. I don't want some gunhand climbing my back because you are worried about Frank."

She fled into the next room.

The remaining men on his side gathered at the edge of the earth-covered potato cellar. One was gesturing towards the two men lying in the open. Luther placed four bullets near the group, one of which he thought hit someone, even at that extreme range.

Frank hurried into the room. "Aunt Kate says

they are moving up on her side, also." To emphasize his report she began to fire sporadically in response to growing sniper fire from outside. The men behind the potato cellar moved in her direction. He helped them along with a couple of near misses.

"You stay here, Frank. I'll send Emily back to help."

Frank put out a hand to stop him. "You don't have to keep someone with me all the time. I'm over that nonsense about giving up."

Luther regarded him for a moment. "I accept that. Don't go feeling you have to prove anything to the rest of us, though. You don't. I want Emily to stay with you because you two are the least experienced. You can help each other."

He moved silently into the next room. Emily was leaning farther and farther out the window, her silhouette plain, as she tracked someone outside. Her rifle fired and Luther dove across the room to pull her clear of the window just before a volley of shots shattered the glass and splintered the frame.

She lay for a moment in surprise, stunned at what she had attracted, staring at the place she had been as bullet after bullet passed through.

"You don't want to let them see too much of you," Luther said mildly. "They are playing for keeps out there."

She smiled weakly up at him. "I think you just saved my life."

"Don't go all gushy on me. Get back in there and help Frank." She crawled slowly towards the door. "Did you get him?" he asked with a smile.

Emily paused and turned her head. "I think I missed. You pulled me away before I could see for sure."

He moved to another window and filled the magazine of his rifle. "When you see something, shoot at it, but keep down. I will be satisfied if you just keep them nervous."

A rifle fired from the next room.

"Get in there and help Frank," he ordered kindly as he turned to the window. A shape lay close to the picket fence. He thought it would be better not to tell her she had hit the man at whom she had shot.

Several men rose from the darkness at the foot of the hill, firing at the house as they zig-zagged towards him. Their bullets thumped wildly into the house, most of them in the west side. They seemed more concerned with the flanking fire Will was directing at them from his second-floor window. One of the approaching men always zigged the same distance for the same length of time. Luther shot him in the middle of his next turn.

The other two dropped into the cover of the brush at the edge of the yard. He could hear them talking back and forth and drove several shots in that direction.

Then they were up again and running, this time towards the hill, their wounded friend swearing angrily at them for leaving him behind.

"Hey!" Luther called.

There was a sudden silence.

"You just as well talk to me, I'm looking right over my front sight and down your throat."

"What do you want?" the man answered, finally.

"Can you move?"

"I suppose so. I'm hit in the leg above the knee. If I can get up, I can hop." He thought a moment. "Why? Would you rather shoot me standing up than lying down?"

Luther chuckled. "If you can get up, get out of there. I'll hold my fire."

The man lay motionless for a long time. "Why you letting me go?" he asked at last.

"Maybe you'll tell Henry it isn't going to work. You're losing too many men and not getting anywhere."

Another prolonged period of silence followed. "What the hell!" the man called finally. "All right. I'm getting up now." Luther watched him struggle to his feet and stand for a moment facing the house. When nothing happened he turned and began to hop slowly towards his friends.

A warm hand touched him on the shoulder. He jerked around, almost knocking Emily over. "There's trouble in the kitchen. Katherine is yelling something terrible." Now that she had brought it to his attention, he could hear the woman's voice above the intermittant rifle fire.

"You stay here. Don't shoot the one hopping away. I told him I would let him go."

He ran through the house to the kitchen to find Katherine confronting a man standing over the body of another lying on the floor. In her hand was a heavy meat cleaver.

Her blouse was torn and her hair hung in strag-

173

gling feathers from the bun she had pinned up in earlier. The man across from her was gaping at her in pure terror. As the cleaver turned, it reflected the faint light and Luther saw it was splotched with fresh blood.

The two were at a stand-off, but Katherine's anger was up. She was taunting him, "Come get what your friend got if you think it's worth it!" Her voice was strange, almost animal.

He crept up behind her and grabbed her, pinning her arms to her sides. "Take your friend and get out," he ordered the frightened man. "Any false moves and I'll let her have you."

The man stared at the woman struggling desperately with Luther and bent to pick up the body from the floor between them. He backed slowly out the door and across the porch, never taking his eyes from the enraged woman.

Luther released her and stepped well back as she turned on him cleaver raised. "You're fantastic, Katherine," he said with a grin.

Her wild eyes gradually calmed and she slumped against the table. "The first one came in through the pantry window while I was watching across the porch. I didn't know he was there until he grabbed me from behind."

She tucked her blouse back in. "I think he was more interested in what he found under my shirt than anything else. I backed across to the sink and while he was exploring me I grabbed the cleaver. You saw the rest." A sudden violent reaction shook her body.

He pulled her close and held her for a long moment until her trembling died away. "You all right now?"

She nodded. "You get back to the front. I don't suppose it is over yet." Before he left, he nailed the pantry window shut.

While he was in this part of the house he checked on Will. The hotelkeeper was enjoying himself. No one had gotten really close. As Luther left, Will was keeping it that way by discouraging a shadow which had moved into range with a couple of well-placed bullets.

The firing outside stopped. When the defenders also stopped shooting, the sudden silence was almost as loud as the constant gunfire had been. He hurried through the house to kneel beside Emily. "What's going on?"

"I don't know for certain, but I think I saw Stiles' buggy arrive a few minutes ago."

The short, thin man who walked out into the open a few minutes later confirmed her observation. "Luther North!" he called. "I want to talk to you."

"Then talk. I can hear you fine."

"This is private. Come out here. I'll guarantee your safety."

"I'll guarantee my own safety by staying in here. What do you want?"

"What would you say to ten thousand dollars?" the banker asked smugly.

"For what?"

"All you have to do is get on your horse and ride out of here. Don't look back."

"Do you really think money would buy me out of here?" Luther's voice reflected his amazement.

"Why not? You've worked for pay before." Stiles was growing more confident the longer Luther let him talk and took a couple of steps forward. The sharp click as Emily cocked her rifle stopped him abruptly.

"Shall I shoot him?" she asked softly.

"Not just yet. Let's hear the rest of it," he whispered back. Loud enough for the banker to hear he called, "What about the others? You going to buy them off too?"

"I'm afraid that isn't possible. I know you would keep your mouth shut. I can't be sure of them."

"My God! Do you really think I would walk out of here and leave the others to die?" Luther was beginning to sound hostile.

"For ten thousand dollars, yes. What do you say?" Stiles wasn't bothered by his anger.

Luther looked over at Emily. "I would say now is the time to shoot him. Have a go at it."

The resulting shell whistled past the banker's ear. He stood for a moment in shocked surprise and then turned and ran wildly for the fence.

"Damn!" Emily said with feeling. "I missed."

Luther chuckled. "You didn't really want to shoot him. Better to let a jury of his peers hang him."

"That is not quite correct," she said primly.

"It might be better for a jury to hang him, but I did want to shoot him. I wanted to very badly. I'm just not very good with one of these things," she admitted regretfully.

Luther sat on the floor and laughed. There was a snort behind him and he turned to find the others standing in the door. "What are you doing here?" he growled half-heartedly. "They could be coming in all around the house."

But they didn't. Only an occasional shot kept those in the house awake for the rest of the night.

CHAPTER NINETEEN

In the dim pre-dawn light, they watched the preparation of the heavy wagon just out of rifle range on the other side of the barn. The end towards the house was fortified with bales of hay to protect the men who were scrambling into the box behind them. A team of draft horses was hitched backwards, nose to the wagon box, so they would be pushing the wagon and be protected from the fire of the defenders.

The way the wagon was aimed indicated the point

of impact would be the corner of the house where the front porch bulged out. If the wagon should make it that far, the men sheltered behind the hay would be able to leap from the wagon to the porch without much chance for the defenders to prevent it.

Then only a single wall would separate them from the attackers. A unified rush would be beyond their ability to repel.

A steady covering fire began from behind the blackened ruins of the barn making it difficult for them to occupy the ground floor windows on that side of the house.

"If we only had something we could hold that wagon away from the house with, we might have a chance," suggested Will.

"I've been through this whole house. There isn't a thing we can use," Luther replied gloomily. "We are just going to have to make them earn this house room by room."

As he stomped around the parlor, what he had just said filtered through his tired mind. "No!" he said explosively. "There is just a chance that with all their men concentrating on that wagon they aren't watching the side of the house towards the hill. Will, you take the others out that side and get away from here. I'll try to hold them up as long as possible. There is no reason for all of us to die here."

"I won't hear of it." Katherine's voice was strained. "Send the young ones out with Will. I intend to stay here with you."

"There might be something we could do," Frank began diffidently.

Luther turned on him. "If you have any ideas at all, now is the time to spit them out. We only have a few minutes left."

"There is a five gallon can of kerosene on the back porch. Maybe we can use it to set the wagon on fire."

Luther was suddenly, totally alert. "Get it and take it up to the room above this. Katherine, you and Emily find all the empty bottles you can. If there is a funnel in the kitchen bring that too." He turned to Will. "You're going to have to appear to be our last line of defense. Keep potting away at whatever shows itself."

He grabbed his rifle and ammunition and hurried upstairs close on the heels of Frank who was dragging the heavy can. The women followed loaded down with bottles. "Fill them up with the kerosene. Use pieces of this curtain as corks." He stepped across to the window facing the wagon and tore the cloth down, the motion attracting a hail of bullets which broke out all the glass.

He had seen a fancy lamp on the shelf in the closet of the master bedroom. It was a blown glass affair, perfect for what he had in mind. He filled the reservoir and lit the wick, setting it so it burned full on. Then he replaced the glass chimney and set it well to one side away from the group working with the kerosene. When he was done, the others had finished filling a half-dozen bottles.

"How is your throwing arm, Frank?" he asked with a grin.

"Pretty good." The boy had finally begun to take an interest in what was happening to them.

"Good. You throw the bottles out over the wagon. I'll break them with the rifle." He glanced out the window and saw the wagon was now beginning its slow approach.

"When I tell you to throw, stay well back in the room. I don't want you getting shot this late in the game. You women stay out of the line of fire, too."

The wagon was now only ten yards away.

"Throw the first one."

The bottle glanced from the side of the window frame and angled away, well clear of the wagon. "I don't think I can do this," Frank began.

"Nonsense," Luther snapped. "You just needed to get the range. We have plenty of bottles and time. You are the only one who can do this, so hang in there."

Frank took a deep breath and launched a second bottle. This one rose in a beautiful arc over the wagon. Luther shattered it with a bullet just as it passed over the hay, soaking the wagon with a splash of kerosene. The men responded with a hail of cursing and bullets aimed at the window.

"As fast as you can throw," Luther ordered. The excited boy responded, bottle following bottle more quickly as he gained confidence. The women kept filling new ones for him and Luther was working the lever on his rifle almost as fast as possible. The swearing men and the wagon were soon soaked with the smelly fluid.

"Hold it," Luther said finally. "That should be enough." He picked up the lamp, checked to see that it was burning properly and threw it into the wagon.

Before the tinkle of breaking glass had died away the flames began to spread rapidly. Screaming men dropped from the wagon and began to roll desperately on the ground in an attempt to put out the flames which ate at their kerosene soaked clothing and hair.

The team of horses tried to back away from the roaring flames under their noses and pulled the blazing wagon away from the house.

They watched the results of their action in awe from the window. Luther put a hand on Frank's shoulder and said with feeling, "I think you have just saved all our lives, Frank. I, for one, am grateful as hell!"

The boy flushed with pleasure and Emily put her arm around him and hugged him tight. "Anyone could have thought of the kerosene. You figured out how to use it." They watched the fire gradually burn itself out and the burned men help each other away.

"But we didn't think of it, Frank. You are the one kept his eyes open. Figuring out how to use it was the easy part." He and Frank leaned farther out the window for a better view of their vanquished foe.

The rifles which had been silent for some time spoke again from their places behind the barn. Frank staggered back, hand pressed suddenly against his shoulder. The look on his face more one of surprise than of pain.

"I've been shot!" he announced in wonder.

Luther grabbed for his rifle as the women led Frank downstairs to a safer place in which to tend his wound.

Before he could open fire he heard a heavier boom from the hill above the house. A grin spread across his face as he also began to fire at the men trying to find cover from this new enemy.

Jester had arrived with his treasured Sharps. It had plenty of range to fire well into what had been safe ground for the gang. They soon decided it was all over, some fleeing on horseback. Several of the wounded and badly burned giving themselves up.

Luther unhitched the horses from the still smouldering wagon and thought over what the prisoners had told him while he waited for Jester to work his way down from the hill.

They had said that just before they were ready to start the assualt, the telegrapher from town had ridden in and talked privately to Stiles and the Sheriff. The two had promised them a bonus for the death of Luther and the others and then gone into town with the messenger. That was partly the reason the last attack had been so slow developing. With no leaders around there had not been a lot of enthusiam for further risk.

When it was clear the fight was really over, Will had ridden into town for the doctor. Katherine had arranged the wounded men along the front porch, and with Emily's help, was tending them as best as she could. As the gang fled, farmers and their wives began to arrive, the women helping nurse and the men standing around and complaining because they hadn't been asked to help.

Jester strutted across the yard, a smile on his

round face, his Sharps cocked over one shoulder. "That banker is all through," he annoucned. "The governor sent out his top man to clean all this up."

The farmers began to gather and Luther led them over to the porch so the women could hear also. Jester was always ready to be the center of attention and his manner puffed up as he explained. "I went first to Jay King's office, like you said in your letter, Luther. I showed it to him and the names made him take me right over to the capitol. Turns out the governor and Frank's father went to school together back east. They had been writing back and forth about the trouble out here for months. He wanted to turn out the militia and really clean this place out."

He looked at Luther smugly. "I told him I figured we could handle it. All he should do was send some-one out here with the authority to stand behind us. He sent Jay. He'll be arriving in Singleshoe on this morning's train. I rode straight through the night so I could be in on the finish. Looks like I got here just in time to save the day."

Katherine snorted in amusement from the porch above and Frank grinned from where he was receiving the personal care of a very solicitous Emily.

Luther turned to the farmers. "Will Karren has gone for the doctor. Would some of you take charge of these men? I need to get into town to meet Jay and see about Stiles. All these men will have to be brought into town when the Doc says they can travel. We don't want any of them to get away before the trial."

As he helped Katherine into the spring wagon, he

said to Jester. "You stay out here and keep an eye on things. This isn't over. Someone warned Stiles and Carr early this morning about the governor's intervention. I have a feeling they've skipped with all the valuables they could carry."

CHAPTER TWENTY

"As far as I'm concerned, Katherine, I think we should leave it to the state to deal with Stiles and Carr."

Luther was seated at a table in the dining room of Will Karren' hotel with her and a balding, older man. They had both had a chance to clean up, change into fresh clothing and eat a good meal.

"Luther's right, Miss Stone," said the baldish man. "I have had a chance to go through most of the bank's papers and there is little doubt in my mind your nephew will get all his property back. You and Luther should take some time for yourselves."

She appeared ready to be convinced. "Please call me Katherine, Mr. King. From what Luther had told me about you I already look upon you as a friend." Her voice hardened slightly, "But you must realized I have to be certain Frank is taken care of and the men who caused all this trouble are punished. I owe that to my brother."

"Stiles and Carr are long gone from this part of the country, Katherine. The only men left from their gang are those who were too badly wounded or burned to escape. I have notified law officers all around the state to be on the lookout for both of the ringleaders. We should have them any time now."

"I suppose you should know as well as anyone." She glanced determindly at Luther. "But I still intend to remain right here in Singleshoe until they are behind bars. Stiles is a devious man. I will believe you have him when I see it."

Luther sighed, "Now, Katherine."

"Aunt Katherine—Mr. North!"

The three turned to stare at the girl standing in the door. Her clothing was wet and badly torn, her hair in tangles, tears were running down her dusty face.

Luther stood abruptly, "What's happened, Emily?"

"They took Frank!" she sobbed.

Katherine rushed across the room to take her by the arm and support her to a seat at the table. "Who took Frank?"

"Mr. Stiles and the Sheriff." The girl was almost

hysterical, her breath coming in short, savage gasps.

Luther poured her a glass of water. "How could they, Emily? You were out at the ranch with Jester." A dark look crossed his face. "If he got to talking and let someone ride right in and take Frank—"

"It wasn't Jester's fault." She used the remains of a torn sleeve to mop at her face, brushed her hair back out of her eyes and tried to regain control of herself.

"Frank and I wanted to be alone so we borrowed a buckboard from one of the farmers." She looked at Katherine as she explained, "I had treated him so badly, and then he got shot. There were so many things we had to talk about and we couldn't do it with all those people around."

Katherine patted her soothingly on the arm. "We understand that, Emily. Just tell us what happened."

"We didn't think there was any danger. The chance that those men might still be around never entered our minds. Frank drove towards town, just poking along, talking."

Luther cleard his throat. "We have also been sitting here assuming they were long gone."

The admission seemed to steady the girl. "There was a stream and a pretty grove of trees just off the road. It looked so peaceful we decided to stop. We were walking down beside the stream, talking and holding hands and then, suddenly, they were there."

She looked at Luther. "They must have been hiding in the grove. Stiles and the Sheriff and three other men. They rode out and formed a semicircle around us, trapping us against the stream. Mr. Stiles seemed like a different man, all rumpled and angry

188

looking.

"The Sheriff said we would be perfect as hostages, no one would dare try anything if they had us along. He got down from his horse and made a grab for me. Frank pushed me towards the stream and told me to run, then he fought them so I could get away. He was so brave!"

There were tears on her cheeks again and Katherine put an arm around her. Emily picked at her wet dress. "I fell down in the water, but I could hear Frank yelling for me to get away, so I got up and ran on into the trees. I guess they decided Frank would be enough of a hostage for them, because they didn't even try to follow me. They put him up on a horse and rode away across the fields. The buckboard was still there, so I drove it into town."

Jester ran into the room and stopped short at sight of Emily. "Thank God you're all right!" He looked around. "They got away with Frank, Luther."

Luther repeated Emily's story for his benefit, finishing with, "You shouldn't have let them come to town alone. I told you to keep an eye on them."

"This isn't the moment for that, Luther," King commented. "He couldn't have known Stiles was still around any more than the rest of us did." He turned to the girl. "Did you recognize any of them besides Carr and Stiles?"

"Only that man in the red shirt Mr. North captured on the hill. I hadn't seen the other two before."

Jester offered, "I followed their trail for a ways after I found these two were gone. Frank put up a pretty good scrap, then they took him off into that rough country to the west where I lost their tracks on hard ground. I figured it would be best to come into town and tell you, so I didn't try to pick up the trail again."

Luther looked at Katherine. "Stiles might have a place in that broken country west of here he would use in an emergency. Is there any chance his wife would know where it is?"

"Would she tell if she did?" King asked.

"She'll tell," Katherine stated.

Matilda Stiles looked at each member of the group which confronted her in turn. "Can't you leave me alone? I had nothing to do with any of this. You have to believe I didn't know what Benton was doing."

There was something a bit wrong with her eyes. They didn't quite focus anywhere and seemed larger than normal. Her voice was also strange, as if she had to focus for any sound to come. As they approached across the room she retreated into a corner.

Luther stopped just out of reach. "We need to know if your husband has a place out in that rough country the other side of the Weston place."

"I don't know," she muttered. "I don't know anything about it."

She reached out suddenly and grasped Katherine's arm. "You remember me from when we were girls together, Kate. What will I do now? What will people say?"

Katherine freed herself from the hand. "You can help us, Matilda. Tell Luther if your husband has a cabin or ranch west of here."

"I don't know anything about any of this," she screamed. "Can't you leave me alone? Things were going so well and then that fool had to go and do this. Why couldn't he have considered what it would do to our good name?"

"Damn!" Jester whispered. "She's going crazy!"

Emily had gone upstairs to change into a clean dress. She returned leading May by the hand.

Matilda Stiles jerked upright. "Don't let her see me like this. She mustn't know what has happened."

May ran across to her mother and put her arms around her waist. "Don't cry, Mama. It will be all right." The little girl looked around at the others. "Don't hurt her. She's my mother!" Matilda was trembling badly.

Katherine put an arm around her tenderly and said softly, "You want May to go to Laurel Heights, don't you, Matty?"

The woman nodded, unable to reply.

"If you tell us where your husband has gone, I will promise to see she is admitted there and has the best possible care."

"She can live with me, Mrs. Stiles," Emily offered.

Matilda Stiles made an effort to regain control. "What was it you wanted to know?"

"Is there any kind of cabin or ranch your husband might use at a time like this in that country west of here?"

She nodded, finally. "He did talk about a small cabin back in the canyon country."

CHAPTER TWENTY-ONE

Luther and Jester lay on their stomachs and peered cautiously over the rim of the canyon at the cabin far below. Their vantage point more than a hundred feet above the floor at the closed end of the box canyon confirmed it to be a perfect defensive position for Stiles and Carr and the other men who had shut themselves inside.

The narrow canyon extended straight east from the cabin for almost two hundred yards with no stone or bush to provide cover for anyone approaching. The walls of the canyon were perpendicular offering them no path of descent. At the far end of the straight approach the canyon bent sharply north and then again eastward preventing sight of the cabin from the larger canyon of which this was a narrow offshoot.

Luther had hoped there might be a chance of forcing the gang out into the open by setting the cabin roof on fire with dropped torches. Jester had brough him up here so he would be better able to assess the cabin's defenses for himself.

"I spent a week here with Old Armin Dopps back in fifty-six," his friend explained. "He had been holed up here for more than ten years working on this place. Every time he killed an attacker he would cut off his head and put the skull on the front edge of the roof, the eyes looking down the canyon. I don't mind telling you, riding in there was about all my nerves could stand with all them empty eye sockets staring at me."

Luther took another look at the cabin illuminated by the light of the almost full moon. "It does look like he was afraid of something. That place is a fortress."

Jester drew back from the edge. 'I best tell you about Old Armin. It might help you figure a way in, though the entire Utah nation spent close on ten years at it without much success."

They moved back to where the two farmers who had accompanied them to the top of the mountain were waiting. Three more were camped in the mouth of the canyon to make sure the gang stayed bottled up inside. The five wanted to be in on the capture of Stiles because of their friends who had been forced to flee their homes in the night.

Using a large boulder for a backrest and working slowly at filling his ancient pipe, Jester began. "I first met Old Armin down to Bent's just after he had come out from the east. He wasn't a very sociable man, but then a lot of us back in those days were out here because we couldn't quite deal with society. I rode west with him as far as the *Fontaine-qui-bouille* which I followed on up the front range. He crossed on over into *Bayou Salado* and fell in with a small band of Utes who took pity on him and saw to it he survived the winter. Then he killed the son of one of their medicine men over something foolish and managed to enrage the rest of the tribe into swearing a vendetta against him. They chased him east until he stumbled on that canyon down below us. There is a small spring behind the cabin and I always kind of suspected his horse found it, not him. Anyway, he managed to hold the Indians off long enough to get his defenses built.

"He knew they would be back with help, so he picked that canyon clear of every loose rock and used them to build his cabin walls. In the front there are three slits which are only four inches wide on the outside, but fan out on the inside so he could command the entire canyon with his rifle. The door is set in the back with only a foot wide passage between the cabin wall and the cliff leading to it. He built kind of an overhang so he could dump boiling water on anyone who came down that passage. Told me he

194

got the idea from reading about old crusader castles when he was young.

"The only wood in the place is the beams which hold up the roof. He spent months finding and dragging in heavy slabs of slate for that roof so it would be both fireproof and strong." Jester finally lit the pipe he had been holding. "That's why I said it would be impossible for you to burn Stiles out of there."

"How did the Indians finally get him?"

"They didn't. Tried for a long time, but when he had a whole row of skulls along the front of the roof they finally decided enough was enough. Not that they didn't drop by once in a while just on the off chance he was out where they could get at him."

"Then what happened to him?" one of the farmers asked.

"That's why I spent the week there. A message came into Bent's while I was spending the summer with some Arapahoe and Bill recalled I knew Armin slightly. Everyone knew his story and where he was forted up, but he wouldn't let anyone approach unless he knew them. Armin was a bit nervous about strangers. Bill figured I could convince him to let me in. I did and it turned out his older brother had died childless and left him his estate. Me and the Arapahoe gave him an escort clear out to the Republican before he felt safe enough to go on alone. Never heard of him after that."

There was a long silence before Luther asked, "Can we wait them out?"

"Not if they have any supplies. Old Armin built

that cabin right up against the mouth of the spring. Hollowed out a cave back into the cliff for a storage room and final refuge. The Utes sometimes kept him penned up in there five—six months at a time."

Luther crawled back out and looked over the edge again. "I still think the roof is the weak point." He came back and stood for a moment in thought. Then he walked slowly around the boulder the old man was using for a backrest.

"Ezra," he ordered with a growing smile. "Go back down to the horses and fetch back all our rope and the shovel and ax off the pack horse. Bring everyone back with you except Wat. Tell him to stay alert in the canyon."

When the man left he nudged at the boulder and nodded in satisfaction. "I think this should do the trick."

Jester stood beside him. "What you got in mind, Luther?"

"We are going to drop this boulder through the roof of that cabin."

Jester considered it. "Could kill Frank as easy as any of the others," he commented.

"I'm going to go down and check where he is before we drop it." He led the old man and the other farmer down the slight incline towards a stand of trees. "We are going to need some strong poles."

It was two hours work digging around the base of the five foot diameter rock, prying it out of its hole and then manhandling it up to the canyon rim where it was poised directly above the cabin. They wedged the end of a sturdy pole under the boulder and placed a thick log for a fulcrum so it would only take the muscle of a couple of men to tip it over the edge.

Luther then tied several lengths of rope together, one end around his waist, the other to the saddle of their strongest horse. "When I get done on the roof, all but Erza and Carl go back to the mouth of the canyon. I will signal Jester when I want the rock dropped. He will wave a torch so you can see from up here. Be patient. It could take quite a while."

The horse backed slowly up the incline, lowering him towards the cabin. The overhang of the cliff was enough he had nothing against which to steady himself, so he jerked and spun as the knots in the rope caught and released on the lip of the canyon. He landed lightly on the stone roof, untied the rope, jerked on it twice to signal to those above and watched it rapidly disappear out of sight.

The roof gave slightly under his weight, so, worried that one of the beams might be cracked, he crept to the edge where the thick rock walls would easily bear his weight. He moved along the wall to the front until he was directly above one of the rifle ports. When he leaned out he could see a dim light inside.

Henry Carr was speaking, "...no reason to keep him locked up in that cave. He can't try anything all tied up like he is and it's cold back there. He could catch pneumonia."

A voice rumbled in reply from the back end and, though Luther couldn't quite catch the words, the authority it held over Henry indicated it belonged to Stiles.

The Sheriff answered, "No, I would say there is little danger of that. They couldn't get close enough to place a charge and the canyon wall hangs out enough above us, I doubt they could drop one on the roof. Besides, we're getting out of here when the moon goes down. I intend to live a long life in Canada on my share of this money and no gunfighter is going to stop me."

Luther moved back from the edge using a round rock on the roof for a handhold. He looked down at the off-white object and jerked back when he found himself staring into the empty eye sockets of one of Armin Dopps' Indian skulls.

He then checked the back of the roof on the chance there was a way in and found Dopps had done a beautiful job of fitting the roof slates into a notch cut in the rock face of the cliff. Luther settled down with his back to the rock to wait until he was sure Jester and the others had time to return to the mouth of the canyon.

When he decided it had been long enough he followed the wall out to the front again and, striking a match on his rough jeans, lit a paper spill which he held in the air for several moments before dropping it onto the roof. Almost at once a blazing brand waved in an arc in the mouth of the canyon.

One of the men below him in the cabin murmured something and fired at the light.

Luther drew his revolver and ran back to the rock face to lie flat at the edge of the roof. There was no predicting where the boulder would land.

A rushing sound filled the air and the heavy granite boulder struck the roof just inside the front wall, bursting through the slate. The resulting shock wave rippled across the roof, splintering the slate and shaking Luther badly.

Inside, the rock rattled and crashed around, shattering what furniture there was and bringing surprised yells as the men inside tried to get out of its way.

He crept across to the hole and knelt to peer through.

The room was filled with a cloud of displaced dust and the pieces of the roof which were still falling at random. He could hear the men hacking and coughing as they tried to figure out just what had happened.

Directly below him the floor was clear, the boulder having finally come to rest against the far wall.

Placing a hand on the edge of the hole for balance he dropped through to land in a crouch on the littered floor. He moved quickly out of the shaft of moonlight towards the darkness at the rear of the room.

The dust was still so thick in the air it was difficult to make out everything in the room. Over beside where the boulder had come to rest a man was moaning in pain. Otherwise Luther couldn't see any of the gang.

Carr called across the room. "Somebody watch outside. North'll be trying to get in before we can organize ourselves."

A shape moved between Luther and the narrow

slit of light from a window. He drove a shot into the indistinct figure and stepped quickly to one side.

Someone yelled in fear, "One of them is inside already!" The man fired from where Jester had said the outside door would be.

Luther directed a bullet in that direction and took another step to his left. His boot caught under the soft body of a man lying on the floor who grabbed his leg and pulled him to his knees.

He struck out savagely at where he judged the man's head to be. A solid thunk finally rewarded his repeated lunges and the grip around his leg relaxed.

Crawling along the floor he came to a stone wall which was cold to the touch. It had to be the one between the cabin and the cave with the spring. It had to be the one between the cabin and the cave with the spring. He followed along the wall until he came to a heavy plank door, a sturdy bar secure in its brackets. The bar scraped loudly when he lifted it free and a shot sang across the room.

He flung the heavy bar at the muzzle flash and was violently driven backwards as the door burst open and a familiar figure filled the lighter square of the opening.

"Down, Jester!" he yelled urgently and the figure dropped as men fired from two places in the room.

A gun answered from outside one of the rifle slits and a man screamed in pain over near the boulder. Luther drove three shots at the second man and dropped to the floor. There was a short burst of confused firing, and then suddenly, silence reigned in the smoke and dust filled room.

As he carefully reloaded his gun in the dark, a hand startled him when it dropped onto his leg. "That you. Luther?" Jester whispered.

"Yes. Go outside and see if you can show some light in here."

A moment later a lantern appeared in one of the window slits, casting a dim light across the room.

"Give it up," Jester called. "You ain't got a chance."

Only one member of the gang remained upright. Henry Carr looked around the room, shrugged in resignation and tossed his revolver into the ragged circle of moonlight which steamed in through the hole in the roof. He followed it, hands in the air. "I'm finished. Hold your fire," he pleaded.

Luther stood and walked towards him. Along the back wall another door creaked open and the barrel of a pistol lined up on his back.

A heavy thud forced the door open wider, and Frank, hands and feet bound, tumbled into the main room, knocking Benton Stiles' gun to one side just as it fired. The bullet narrowly missed Luther, whining as it ricocheted from stone wall to stone wall until it finally found its way out of the cabin.

The door slammed shut behind Frank and they could hear the bar drop on the other side. He ran across and pulled at the handle. It wouldn't budge. The door itself was built of two inch thick planks so there was no way they were going to break it down with the tools they had.

He bent to cut Frank loose and helped him out the door as two of the farmers and Jester entered to secure the Sheriff and his men. Frank walked up and down until the circulation returned to his arms and legs then they went back inside to find two of the farmers tending a wounded man while the others kept an eye on Henry Carr.

The man in the red shirt was dead on the floor, his legs crushed by the boulder, his head split open by Luther. In the corner behind the boulder, a man Luther hadn't seen before was dead of several gunshot wounds.

They carried the bodies and the wounded man outside, well clear of the cabin whose roof seemed about ready to collapse.

Jester, Frank and Luther contemplated the door to the cave through two of the window slits. "We could just block it up and leave him," suggested the old man hopefully.

"No," Luther said. "He should stand trial. Is there any other way out of there?" he asked Frank.

"Not that I saw."

They all turned to look back down the canyon as a buggy rattled around the sharp bend. Jay King was driving with Katherine and Matilda Stiles as passengers.

Katherine's eyes searched for Luther among those still standing and the tenseness went out of her body when she found him. She climbed down and hugged Frank. "Are you all right?"

The boy nodded. "Where's Emily?"

"She stayed in Singleshoe to take care of May."

"Did Stiles get away?" Jay asked.

"Locked himself in a cave behind the cabin. We

haven't figured how to get him out yet."

After looking at the shambles inside the cabin, and the huge boulder which rested against one wall, Jay commented, "I remembered about Dopps and his cabin after you were on your way and didn't think you would be able to get in. I see I underestimated you, Luther." He indictaed the woman standing stiffly beside the buggy. "Mrs. Stiles agreed to come out and try to talk her husband into giving up."

"If she can talk him out of that cave it will save us a lot of trouble."

Jay walked across to the woman and spoke quietly for a moment. She nodded curtly a couple of times and moved inside to the heavy door, right hand buried deep in the pocket of her skirt.

She rapped on the door with her left hand and called, mouth close to the crack where the door met the jamb, "Benton. It's me. Mat. Let me come in and talk to you."

They could all hear the faint murmer of a voice answering. She looked around. "They are all well back, Benton. Let me in. No one will try anything."

The bar scraped across the rough wood and Jester took a step forward. Luther put out a hand to restrain him. "Not yet. Let her talk to him first."

The door cracked open and she slipped inside. Stiles locked it again behind her.

Katherine came over and slipped a hand into one of Luther's, standing close for comfort.

After several moments of silence Matilda's voice could be heard, much too shrill to be understood by those outside.

Then four very clear words from Stiles. "My God! Matilda! No!"

A single shot...

A long silence...

A second shot...

And the door swung slowly open.

Matilda Stiles stood there, a faint ribbon of powder smoke rising from the revolver she held in her hand.

Her eyes searched for and found Katherine. "Make sure my May goes to Laurel Heights. Will you promise me that?"

Katherine, unable to speak, nodded.

Matilda Stiles raised the pistol to her head. "He shouldn't have taken away my good name."

She pulled the trigger.

CHAPTER TWENTY-TWO

The engineer was walking around his engine with
an oil can and a rag making sure the powerful
Baldwin American was ready to continue its journey
eastward. The chuffing as the compressor kept the
reservoir of the Westinghouse brake system filled
and the occasional spurts of steam as the overload
valves released excess pressure set the tone for the
group on the platform beside the through Pullman.

May Stiles had been hugged by Katherine and
handed up to the porter who led her inside so the

others could say their farewells.

Emily was moist-eyed and Frank was trying to be very casual and adult. The only relaxed members of the group were Katherine and Luther.

"I will write your mother a letter about May and the Stiles'" Katherine said. "Let Elizabeth take care of her. You and Frank have earned the chance for a more private beginning for your marriage."

"We won't have any problems, Aunt Katherine. There is enough love around our house to raise May right." Emily took Luther's hand in her's and stated, "I still don't understand why Mrs. Stiles killed herself. From what mother had told me about her, she would have been the last person I would have expected to do that."

"I think it was probably the shock from the loss of all she had worked and driven her husband to achieve. She wasn't ready to face being the wife of an imprisoned man. She hoped no blame would fall on May when she grew up if neither of her parents were around to be remembered."

Katherine nodded in agreement. "I think she had come to live for the little girl's future. When she was in school with me, she had big plans for her own life. It was all she ever talked about; money, society, her good name. When she married Stiles, she thought he could give her all that. Instead, he brought her out here. Singleshoe wasn't the town of her dreams, so she focused on May's in their place. When she found out the truth about her husband it left her with nothing to live for."

"Besides," Luther commented. "She knew all her

old school friends would band together to take care of May if she was an orphan. If Matilda remained alive she wasn't sure they would accept the child."

Katherine smiled. "She was probably right in that, anyway." She kissed Frank. "I will make sure Franklin's estate is settled as quickly as possible and sent on to you. Mr. King thinks he has a buyer for the farm already."

While Katherine said goodbye to Emily, Luther led Frank to one side. "I know you have had your doubts about your behavior out here. Wondered whether you were man enough to stand up to this kind of life. I don't think you have to worry any longer. You fought for Emily and you saved my life. As far as I'm concerned, you've proven your courage. You can ride with me anytime." He shook his hand firmly. "I'm glad to have known you, Frank."

The conductor interrupted, "Best be getting on board, folks."

Frank helped Emily up the steps to the platform and then turned to hug his aunt one last time. "What are your plans when you are finished here?"

She looked over to where Luther waited at one side, an intriguing smile on her face. "I plan to go swimming in a pond."